THE LUCK OF LORNE

A great war sword, seven hundred years old, has been missing for over a hundred years from its niche in the Long Hall of Pirate's Haven, the Ralestones' Louisiana Plantation.

It is a sword of magic powers, brought home from the Crusades.

Since it disappeared, the Ralestones have not prospered. Now, the present generation means to find it . . . if they can foil the schemes of those who mean them harm.

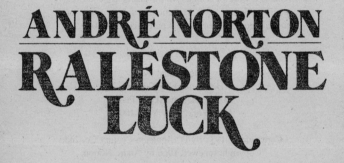

ANDRÉ NORTON
RALESTONE LUCK

A DELL/EMERALD BOOK

Published by
Dell Publishing Co., Inc.
1 Dag Hammarskjold Plaza
New York, New York 10017

Dell ® TM 681510, Dell Publishing Co., Inc.

ISBN: 0-440-07265-4

Printed in the United States of America
First printing—June 1984

TO
D. B. N.
*In return for
many miles of proof
so diligently read*

CONTENTS

1

THE RALESTONES COME HOME

Once upon a time two brave princes and a beautiful princess set out to make their fortunes—'' began the dark-haired, dark-eyed boy by the convertible.

"Royalty is out of fashion," corrected Ricky Ralestone somewhat indifferently. "Can't you do better than that?" She gave her small, pert hat an exasperated tweak which brought the unoffending bowl-shaped bit of white felt into its proper position over her right eyebrow. "How long does it take Rupert to ask a single simple question?"

Her brother Val watched the gas gage on the instrument board of the convertible fluctuate wildly as the attendant of the station shook the hose to speed the flow of the last few drops. Five gallons—did he have enough to pay for it? He began to assemble various small hoards of change from different pockets.

"Do you think we're going to like this?" Ricky waved her hand vaguely in a gesture which included a dilapidated hot-dog stand and a stretch of road white-hot under the steady baking of the sun.

"Well, I think that Pirate's Haven is slightly different from our present surroundings. Where's your proper pride? Not everyone can be classed among the New Poor," Val observed judiciously.

"Nobility in the bread line." His sister sniffed with what she fondly believed was the air of a Van Astor dowager.

"Nobility?"

"We never relinquished the title, did we? Rupert's still the Marquess of Lorne."

"After some two hundred years in America I am afraid that we would find ourselves strangers in England. And Lorne crumbled to dust long ago."

"But he's still Marquess of Lorne," she persisted.

"All right. And what does that make you?"

"Lady Richanda, of course, silly. Can't you remember the wording of the old charter? And you're Viscount—"

"Wrong there," Val corrected her. "I'm only a lord, by courtesy, unless we can bash Rupert on the head some dark night and chuck him into the bayou."

"Lord Valerius." She rolled it upon her tongue.

"Marquess, Lady, and Lord Val, out to seek their fortunes. Pity we can't do it in the traditional family way."

"But we can't, you know," he protested laughingly. "I believe that piracy is no longer looked upon with favor by the more solid members of any community. Though plank-walking is an idea to keep in mind when the bill collectors start to draw in upon us."

"Here comes Rupert at last. Rupert," she raised her voice as their elder brother opened the door by the driver's seat, "shall we all go and be pirates? Val has some lovely gory ideas."

"Not just yet anyway—we still have a roof over our heads," he answered as he slid in behind the wheel. "We should have taken the right turn a mile back."

"Bother!" Ricky surveyed as much of her face as she could see in the postage-stamp mirror of her compact. "I don't think I'm going to like Louisiana."

"Maybe Louisiana won't care for you either," Val offered slyly. "After all, we dyed-in-the-wool Yanks coming to live in the deep South—"

"Speak for yourself, Val Ralestone." She applied a puff carefully to the tip of her upturned nose. "Since we've got this barn of a place on our hands, we might as well live in it. Too bad you couldn't have persuaded our artist tenant to sign another lease, Rupert."

"He's gone to spend a year in Italy. The place is in fairly good condition though. LeFleur said that as long as we don't use the left wing and close off the state bedrooms, we can manage nicely."

"State bedrooms—" Val drew a deep breath which was

3

meant to be one of reverence but which turned into a sneeze as the convertible's wheels raised the dust. "How does it feel to own such magnificence, Rupert?"

"Not so good," he replied honestly. "A house as big as Pirate's Haven is a burden if you don't have the cash to keep it up properly. Though this artist chap did make a lot of improvements on his own."

"But think of the Long Hall—" began Ricky, rolling her eyes heavenward.

"And just what do you know about the Long Hall?" demanded Rupert.

"Why, that's where dear Great-great-uncle Rick's ghost is supposed to walk, isn't it?" she asked innocently. "I hope that our late tenant didn't scare him away. It gives one such a blue-blooded feeling to think of having an active ghost on the premises. A member of one's own family, too!"

"Sure. Teach him—or it—some parlor tricks and we'll show it—or him—off every afternoon between three and four. We might even be able to charge admission and recoup the family fortune," Val suggested brightly.

"Have you no reverence?" demanded his sister. "And besides, ghosts only walk at night."

"Now that's something we'll have to investigate," Val interrupted her. "Do ghosts have union rules? I mean, I wouldn't want Great-great-uncle Rick to march up and down the carriage drive with a sign reading, 'The Ralestones are unfair to ghosts,' or anything like that."

"We'll have to use the Long Hall, of course," cut in Rupert, as usual ignoring their nonsense. "And the old summer drawing-room. But we can shut up the dining-room and the ball-room. We'll eat in the kitchen, and that and a bedroom apiece—"

"I suppose there are bathrooms, or at least a bathroom," his brother interrupted. "Because I don't care to rush down to the bayou for a good brisk plunge every time I get my face dirty."

"Harrison put in a bathroom at his own expense last fall."

"For which blessed be the name of Harrison. If he hadn't gone to Italy, he would have rebuilt the house. How soon do we get there? This touring is not what I thought it might be—"

The crease which had appeared so recently between Rupert's eyes deepened.

"Let hurt, Val?" he asked quietly, glancing at the slim figure sharing his seat.

"No. I'm expressing curiosity this time, old man, not just a whine. But if we're going to be this far off the main highway—"

"Oh, it's not far from the city road. We ought to be seing the gate-posts any moment now."

"Prophet!" Ricky leaned forward between them. "See there!"

Two gray stone posts, as firmly planted by time as the avenue of live-oaks they headed, showed clearly in the afternoon light. And from the nearest, deep carven in the stone, a jagged-toothed skull, crowned and grinning, stared blankly at the three in the shabby car. Beneath it ran the insolent motto of an ancient and disreputable clan, "What I want—I take!"

"This is the place all right—I recognize Joe there." Val pointed to the crest. "Good old Joe, always laughing."

Ricky made a face. "Horrid old thing. I don't see why we couldn't have had a swan or something nice to swank about."

"But then the Lords of Lorne were hardly a nice lot in their prime," Val reminded her. "Well, Rupert, let's see the rest."

The car followed a graveled drive between tall bushes which would have been the better for a pruning. Then the road made a sudden curve and they came out upon a crescent of lawn bordering upon a stone-paved terrace three steps above. And on the terrace stood the home a Ralestone had not set foot in for over fifty years—Pirate's Haven.

"It looks—" Ricky stared up, "why, it looks just like the picture Mr. Harrison painted!"

"Which proves why he is now in Italy," Val returned. "But he did capture it on canvas."

"Gray stone—and those diamond-paned windows—and that squatty tower. But it isn't like a Southern home at all! It's some old, old place out of England."

"Because it was built by an exile," said Rupert softly. "An exile who loved his home so well that he labored five years in the wilderness to build its duplicate. Those little diamond-paned windows were once protected with shutters an inch thick, and the place was a fort in Indian times. But

6

it is strange to this country. That's why it's one of the show places. LeFleur asked me if we would be willing to keep up the custom of throwing the state rooms open to the public one day a month.''

"And shall we?" asked Ricky.

"We'll see. Well, don't you want to see the inside as well as the out?"

"Of course! Val, you lazy thing, get out!"

"Certainly, m'lady." He swung open the door and climbed out stiffly. Although he wouldn't have confessed it for any reason, his leg had been aching dully for hours.

"Do you know," Ricky hesitated on the first terrace step, bending down to put aside a trail of morning-glory vine which clutched at her ankle, "I've just remembered!"

"What?" Rupert looked up from the grid where he was unstrapping their luggage.

"That we are the very first Ralestones to—to come home since Grandfather Miles rode away in 1867."

"And why the sudden dip into ancient history?" Val inquired as he limped around to help Rupert.

"I don't know," her eyes were fast upon moss-greened wall and ponderous door hewn of a single slab of oak, "except—well, we are coming home at last. I wonder if—if they know. All those others. Rick and Miles, the first Rupert and Richard and—"

"That spitfire, the Lady Richanda?" Rupert smiled. "Perhaps they do. No, leave the bags here, Val. Let's see the house first."

Together the Ralestones crossed the terrace and came to

stand by the front door which still bore faint scars left by Indian hatchets. But Rupert stooped to insert a very modern key into a very modern lock. There was a click and the door swung inward before his push.

"The Long Hall!" They stood in something of a hesitant huddle at the end of a long stone-floored room. Halfway down its length a wooden staircase led up to the second floor, and directly opposite that a great fireplace yawned mightily, black and bare.

A leather-covered lounge was directly before this, flanked by two square chairs. And by the stairs was an oaken marriage chest. Save for two skin rugs, these were all the furnishings.

But Ricky had crossed hesitatingly to that cavernous fireplace and was standing there looking up as her brothers joined her.

"There's where it was," she said softly and pointed to a deep niche cut into the surface of the stone overmantel. That niche was empty and had been so for more than a hundred years—to their hurt. "That was where the Luck—"

"How hold ye Lorne?" Rupert's softly spoken question brought the well-remembered answer to Val's lips:

"By the oak leaf, by the sea wave, by the broad-sword blade, thus hold we Lorne!"

"The oak leaf is dust," murmured Ricky, "the sea wave is gone, the broadsword is rust, how now hold ye Lorne?"

Her brothers answered her together:

"By our Luck, thus hold we Lorne!"

school, and me—well, out of the plainest hospital bed I ever saw. We've got this house and what Rupert managed to clear from the wreck. Something will turn up. In the meantime—''

"Yes?" she prompted.

"In the meantime," he went on, leaning against the banister for a moment's rest, "we can be looking for the Luck. As Rupert says, we need it badly enough. Here's the upper hall. Which way now?"

"Over to the left wing. These in front are what Rupert refers to as 'state bedrooms.' ''

"Yes?" He opened the nearest door and whistled softly. "Not so bad. About the size of a small union station and provided with all the comforts of a tomb. Decidedly not what we want.''

"Wait, here's a plaque set in the wall. Look!" She ran her finger over a glass-covered square.

"Regulations for guests, or a floor plan to show how to reach the dining-room in the quickest way," her brother suggested.

"No." She read aloud slowly:

" 'THIS ROOM WAS OCCUPIED BY GENERAL
ANDREW JACKSON,
THE VICTOR OF THE BATTLE OF NEW ORLEANS,
UPON THE TENTH DAY AFTER THE BATTLE.' ''

"Whew! 'Old Hickory' here! But I thought that the Ralestones were more or less under a cloud at that time," commented Val.

11

"History—"

"In the making. Quite so. Now may I suggest that we find some slumber rooms slightly more modern? Rupert is apt to become annoyed at undue delay in such matters."

They went down the hall and turned into a short cross corridor. From a round window at the far end a ray of sun still swept in, but it was a sickly, faded ray. The storm Rupert had spoken of could not be far off.

"This is the right way. Mr. Harrison had these little numbers put on the doors for his guests," Ricky pointed out. "I'll take 'three'; that was marked on the plan he sent us as a lady's room. You take that one across the hall and let Rupert have the one next to you."

The rooms they explored were not as imposing as the one which had sheltered Andrew Jackson for a night. Furnished with chintz-covered chairs, solid mahogany bedsteads and highboys, they were pleasant enough even if they weren't chambers to make an antique dealer "Oh!" and "Ah!" Val discovered with approval some stiff prints of mathematically correct clippers hung an exact patterns on his walls, while Ricky's room held one treasure, a dainty dressing-table.

A small door near the end of the hall gave upon a linen closet. And Ricky, throwing her short white jacket and hat upon the chair in her room, set about making beds, having given Val strict orders to return to the lower hall and sort out the luggage before bringing it up.

As he reached the wide landing he stopped a moment. Since that winter night, almost a year in the past, when a passenger plane had decided—in spite of its pilot—to make a landing on a mountainside, he had learned to hobble where he had once run. The accident having made his right leg a rather accurate barometer, that crooked bone was announcing the arrival of the coming storm with a sharp pain or two which shot unexpectedly from knee to ankle. One such caught him as he was about to take a step and threw him suddenly off balance.

He clutched at a dim tapestry which hung across the wall and tumbled through a slit in the fabric—which smelled of dust and moth balls—into a tiny alcove flanking a broad, well-cushioned window-seat under tall windows. Below him in a riot of bushes and hedges run wild, lay the garden. Somewhere beyond must lie Bayou Mercier leading directly to Lake Borgne and so to the sea, the thoroughfare used by their pirate ancestors when they brought home their spoil.

The green of the rank growth below, thought Val, seemed intensified by the strange yellowish light. A moss-grown path led straight into the heart of a jungle where sweet olive, banana trees, and palms grew in a matted mass. Harrison might have done wonders for the house but he had allowed the garden to lapse into a wilderness.

"Val!"

"Coming!" he shouted and pushed back through the curtain. He could hear Rupert moving about the lower hall.

"Just made it in time," he said as the younger Ralestone limped down to join him. "Hear that?"

A steady pattering outside was growing into a wild dash of wind-driven rain. It was dark and Rupert himself was but a blur moving across the hall.

"Do you still have the flash? Might as well descend into the lower regions and put on the lights."

They crossed the Long Hall, passing through another large chamber where furniture huddled under dust covers, and then into a small cupboard-lined passage. This gave upon a dark cavern where Val's hand scraped a table top only too painfully as he went. Then Rupert found the door leading to the cellar, and they went down and down into inky blackness upon which their thread of torchlight made little impression.

The damp, unpleasant scent of mold and wet grew stronger as they descended, and their fingers brushed slime-touched walls.

"Phew! Not very comfy down here," Val protested as Rupert threw the torch beam along the nearest wall. With a grunt of relief he stepped forward to pull open the door of a small black box. "That does it," he said as he threw the switch. "Now for the topside again and some supper."

They negotiated the steps and found the button which controlled the kitchen lights. The glare showed them a room on the mammoth scale suggested by the Long Hall. A giant fireplace still equipped with three-legged pots, toasting irons, and spits was at one side, its brick oven beside it. But a very modern range and sink faced it.

In the center of the room was a large table, while along the far wall were closed cupboards. Save for its size and the novelty of the fireplace, it was an ordinary kitchen, complete to red-checked curtains at the windows. Pleasant and homey, Val thought rather wistfully. But that was before the coming of that night when Ricky walked in the garden and he heard something stir in the Long Hall— which should have been empty—

"Val! Rupert!" A cry which started valiantly became a wail as it echoed through empty rooms. "Where are yo-o-ou!"

"Here, in the kitchen," Val shouted back.

A moment later Ricky stood in the doorway, her face flushed and her usually correct curls all on end.

"Mean, selfish, utterly selfish pigs!" she burst out. "Leaving me all alone in the dark! And it's so dark!"

"We just went down to turn on the lights!" Val began.

"So I see." With a sniff she looked about her. "It took two of you to do that. But it only required one of me to make three beds. Well, this is a warning to me. Next time—" she did not finish her threat. "I suppose you want some supper?"

Rupert was already at the cupboards. "That," he agreed, "is the general idea."

"Beans or—" Ricky's hand closed upon Val's arm with a nipper-like grip. "What," her voice was a thin thread of sound, "was that?"

Above the steady beat of the rain they heard a noise which was half scratch, half thud. Under Rupert's hand the latch of the cupboard clicked.

"Back door," he said laconically.

"Well, why don't you open it?" Ricky's fingers bit tighter so that Val longed to twist out of her grip.

The key grated in the lock and then Rupert shot back the accompanying bolt.

"Something's there," breathed Ricky.

"Probably nothing but a branch blown against the door by the wind," Val assured her, remembering the tangled state of the garden.

The door came back, letting in a douche of cold rain and a black shadow which leaped for the security of the center of the room.

"Look!" Ricky laughed unsteadily and released Val's arm.

In the center of the neat kitchen, spitting angrily at the wet, stood a ruffled and oversized black tom-cat.

2

THE LUCK OF THE LORDS
OF LORNE

"Nice of you to drop in, old man," commented Rupert dryly as he shut the door. "But didn't anyone ever mention to you that gentlemen wipe their feet before entering strange houses?" He surveyed a line of wet paw prints across the brick floor.

"Did he get all wet, the poor little—" Ricky was on her knees, stretching out her hand and positively cooing. The cat put down the paw he had been licking and regarded her calmly out of round, yellow eyes. Then he returned to his washing. Val laughed.

"Evidently he is used to the strong, silent type of human, Ricky. I wonder where he belongs."

"He belongs to us now. Yes him does, doesn't him?" She attempted to touch the visitor's head. His ears went back and he showed sharp teeth in no uncertain manner.

"Better let him alone," advised Rupert. "He doesn't seem to be the kind you can cuddle."

"So I see." Ricky arose to her feet with an offended air. "One would think that I resembled the more repulsive members of my race."

"In the meantime," Rupert again sought the cupboard, "let's eat."

Half an hour later, fed and well content (even Satan, as the Ralestones had named their visitor because of his temperament, having condescended to accept some of the better-done bits of bacon), they sat about the table staring at the dishes. Now it is a very well-known fact that dishes do *not* obligingly leap from a table into a pan of well-soaped water, slosh themselves around a few times, and jump out to do a spot of brisk rubbing down. But how nice it would be if they did, thought Val.

"The dishes—" began Ricky in a faint sort of way.

"Must be done. We gather that. How utterly nasty bacon grease looks when it's congealed." Her younger brother surveyed the platter before him with mournful interest.

"And the question before the house is, I presume, who's going to wash them?" Rupert grinned. "This seems to be as good a time as any to put some sort of a working plan in force. There is a certain amount of so-called housework which has to be done. And there are three of us to do it. It's up to us to apportion it fairly. Shall we say, let everyone care for his or her own room—"

"There are also the little matters of washing, and ironing, and cleaning," Ricky broke in to remind him.

"And we're down to fifty a month in hard cash. But the tenant farmer on the other side of the bayou is to supply us with fresh fruit and vegetables. And our wardrobes are fairly intact. So I think that we can afford to hire the washing done. We'll take turns cooking—"

"Who's elected to do the poisoning first?" Val inquired with interest. "I trust we possess a good cook-book?"

"Well, I'll take breakfast tomorrow morning," Rupert volunteered. "Anyone can boil coffee and toast bread. As for dishes, we'll all pitch in together. And suppose we start right now."

When the dishes were back again in their neat piles on the cupboard shelves, Ricky vanished upstairs, to come trailing down again in a house-coat which she fondly imagined made her look like one of the better-known screen sirens. The family gathered in an aimless way before the empty fireplace of the Long Hall. Rupert was filling a black pipe which allowed him to resemble—in very slight degree, decided Val—an explorer in an English tobacco advertisement. Val himself was stretched full length on the couch with about ten pounds of cat attempting to rest on his center section in spite of his firm refusal to allow the same.

"Br-r-r!" Ricky shivered. "It's cold in here."

"Probably just Uncle Rick passing through—not the weather. No, cat, you may not sit on that stomach. It's just

as full of bacon as yours is and it wants a nice long rest."
Val swept Satan off to the floor and he resignedly went to
roost by the boy's feet in spite of the beguiling noises
Ricky made to attract his attention.

"These stone houses are cold." Rupert scratched a
match on the sole of his shoe. "We ought to have flooring
put down over this stone paving. I saw some wood stacked
up in an outhouse when I put the car away. We'll have it
in tomorrow and see what we can do about a fire in the
evening."

"And I thought the South was always warm." Ricky
examined her hands. "Whoever," she remarked pleasantly,
"took my hand lotion better return it. The consequences
might not be very attractive."

"Are you sure you packed it this morning?" Val asked.

"But of—" Her fingers went to her mouth. "I wonder
if I did? I've just got to have some. We'll drive to town
tomorrow and get a bottle."

"Thirty miles or so for one bottle of gooey stuff," Val
protested.

"Good idea." Rupert stood with his back to the fireplace as if there really were a flame or two within its black
emptiness. "I've some papers that LeFleur wants to see.
Then there're our boxes at the freight station to arrange
transportation for, and we'll have to see about getting a
newspaper and—"

"Make a list," murmured his brother.

Rupert dropped down upon the wide arm of Ricky's
chair and with her only too willing aid set to work. Val
eyed them drowsily. Rupert and Ricky—or to give her her

very formal name in full—Richanda Anne, were "Red" Ralestones, possessing the thin, three-cornered faces, the dark mahogany hair, the sharply defined cheekbones which had been the mark of the family as far back in history as portraits or written descriptions existed. The "Red" Ralestones were marked also by height and a suppleness of body and movement. The men had been fine swordsmen, the ladies noted beauties. But they were also cursed, Val remembered vividly, with uncertain tempers.

Rupert had schooled himself to the point where his emotions were mastered by his will. But Val had seen Ricky enjoy full tantrums, and the last occasion was not so long ago that the scene had become misty in his memory. Generous to the point of self-beggary, loyal to a fault, and incurably romantic, that was a "Red" Ralestone.

Val himself was a "Black" Ralestone, which was a very different thing. They were a new growth on the family tree, a growth which appeared after the Ralestones had been exiled to colonial America. His black hair, his long, dark face of no particular beauty marked with straight, black brows set in a perpetual frown—that was the sign of a "Black" Ralestone. They were as strong-willed as the "Reds," but their anger could be controlled to icy rage.

"Now that you have spent the monthly income," Val suggested as Rupert added up a long column of minute figures scrawled across the first page of his pocket notebook, "let's really get away from economics for one evening. The surroundings suggest something more romantic than dollars and cents. After all, when did a pirate ever show a saving disposition? Would the first Roderick—"

21

"The Roderick who brought home the Luck?" Ricky laughed. "But he brought home a fortune, too, didn't he, Rupert?"

Her brother relit his pipe. "Yes, but a great many lords came home from the Crusades with their pockets filled. Sir Roderick de la Stone thought the Luck worth his entire estate even after he was made Baron Ralestone."

Ricky shivered delicately. "Not altogether nice people, those ancestors of ours," she observed.

"No," Val grinned. "By rights this room should be full of ghosts instead of the beat of just one. How many Ralestones died violently? Seven or eight, wasn't it?"

"But the ones who died in England should haunt Lorne," argued Ricky, half seriously.

"Well then, that sort of confines us to the crews of the ships our great-great-great-grandfather scuttled," her brother replied.

"Rupert," Ricky turned and asked impulsively, "do you really believe in the Luck?"

Rupert looked up at the empty niche. "I don't know— No, I don't. Not the way that Roderick and Richard and all the rest did. But something that has seven hundred years of history behind it—that means a lot."

" 'Then did he take up ye sword fashioned by ye devilish art of ye East from two fine blades found in ye tomb,' " Val quoted from the record of Brother Anselm, the friar who had accompanied Sir Roderick on his crusading. "Do you suppose that that part's true? Could the Luck have been made from two other swords found in an old tomb?"

"Not impossible. The Saracens were master metal workers. Look at the Damascus blades."

"It all sounds like a fairy-tale," commented Ricky. "A sword with magic powers beaten out of two other swords found in a tomb. And the whole thing done under the direction of an Arab astrologer."

"You've got to admit," broke in Val, "that Sir Roderick had luck after it was given to him. He came home a wealthy man and he died a Baron. And his descendants even survived the Wars of the Roses when four-fifths of the great English families were wiped out."

" 'And fortune continued to smile,' " Rupert took up the story, " 'until a certain wild Miles Ralestone staked the Luck of his house on the turn of a card—and lost.' "

"O-o-oh!" Ricky squirmed forward in her chair. "Now comes the pirate. Tell us that, Rupert."

"You know the story by heart now," he objected.

"We never heard it here, where some of it really happened. Tell it, please, Rupert!"

"In your second childhood?" he asked.

"Not out of my first yet," she answered promptly. "Pretty please, Rupert."

"Miles Ralestone, Marquess of Lorne," he began, "rode with Prince Rupert of the Rhine. He was a notorious gambler, a loose liver, and a cynic. And he even threw the family Luck across the gaming table."

" 'The Luck went from him who did it no honor,' " Val repeated slowly. "I read that in that old letter among your papers, Rupert."

"Yes, the Luck went from him. He survived Marston

23

Moor; he survived the death of his royal master, Charles
the First, on the scaffold. He lived long enough to witness
the return of the Stuarts to England. But the Luck was
gone, and with it the good fortune of his line. Rupert, his
son, was but a penniless hanger-on at the royal court; the
manor of Lorne a fire-gutted wreckage.

"Rupert followed James Stuart from England when
that monarch became a fugitive to escape the wrath of his
subjects. And the Marquess of Lorne sank to the role of
pot-house bully in the back lanes of Paris."

"And then?" prompted Val.

"And then a miracle occurred. Rupert was employed by
his master on a secret mission to London, and there the
Luck came again into his hands. Perhaps by murder. But
he died miserably enough of a heavy cold got by lying in a
ditch to escape Dutch William's soldiers."

" 'So is this perilous Luck come again into our hands.
Then did I persevere to mend the fortunes of my house.'
That's what Rupert's son Richard wrote about the Luck,"
Ricky recalled. "Richard, the first pirate."

"He did a good job of fortune mending," commented
Val dryly. "Married one of the wealthiest of the French
king's wards and sailed for the French West Indies all in a
fortnight. Turned pirate with the approval of the French
and took to lifting the cargoes of other pirates."

"I'll bet that most of his success was due to the Lady
Richanda," observed Ricky. "She sailed with him dressed
in man's clothes. Remember that miniature of her that we
saw in New York, the one in the museum? All the 'Black'
Ralestones are supposed to look like her. Hear that, Val?"

"At least it was the Lady Richanda who persuaded her husband to settle ashore," said Rupert. "She was personally acquainted with Bienville and Iberville who were proposing to rule the Mississippi valley for France by building a city near the mouth of the river. And 'Black Dick,' the pirate, obtained a grant of land lying along Lake Borgne and this bayou. Although the city was not begun until 1724, this house was started in 1710 by workmen imported from England.

"The house of an exile," Rupert continued slowly. "Richard Ralestone was born in England, but he left there in his tenth year. In spite of the price on his head, he crept back to Devon in 1709 to see Lorne for the last time. And it was from the rude sketches he made of ruined Lorne that Pirate's Haven was planned."

"Why, we saw those sketches!" Ricky's eyes shone with excitement. "Do you remember, Val?"

Her brother nodded. "Must have cost him plenty to do it," he replied. "Richard had an immense personal fortune of his own gained from piracy, and he spared no expense in building. The larger part of the stone in these walls was brought straight from Europe, just as they later brought the paving blocks for the streets of New Orleans. When he had done—and the place was five years a-building because of Indian troubles and other disturbances—he settled down to live in feudal state. Some of his former seamen rallied around him as a guard, and he imported blacks from the islands to work his indigo fields.

"The family continued to prosper through both French and Spanish domination until the time of American rule."

"Now for Uncle Rick." Ricky settled herself with a wriggle. "This is even more exciting than Pirate Dick."

"In the year 1788, the time of the great fire which destroyed over half of New Orleans, twin boys were born at Pirate's Haven. They came into their heritage early, for their parents died of yellow fever when the twins were still small children.

"Those were restless times. New Orleans was full of refugees. From Haiti, where the revolting blacks were holding a reign of terror, and from France, where to be a noble was to be a dead one, came hundreds. Even members of the royal house, the Duc d'Orleans and his brother, the Duc de Montpensier, came for a space in 1798.

"The city had always been more or less lawless and intolerant of control. Like the New Englanders of the eighteenth century, many respected merchants were also smugglers."

"And pirates," suggested Val.

"The king of smugglers was Jean Lafitte. His forge—where his slaves shaped the wrought-iron which was one of the wonders of the city—was a fashionable meeting-place for the young bloods. He was the height of wit and fashion—daring openly to placard the walls of the town with his notices of smugglers' sales.

"And Roderick Ralestone, the younger of the twins, became one of Lafitte's men. In spite of the remonstrances of his brother Richard, young Rick withdrew to Barataria with Dominique You and the rest of the outlawed captains.

"In the winter of 1814 matters came to a head. Richard wanted to marry an American girl, the daughter of one of

Governor Claiborne's friends. Her father told him very pointedly that since the owners of Pirate's Haven seemed to be indulging in law breaking, such a marriage was out of the question. Aroused, Richard made a secret inspection of certain underground storehouses which had been built by his pirate great-grandfather and discovered that Rich had put them in use again for the very same purpose for which they had been first intended—the storing of loot.

"He waited there for his brother, determined to have it decided once and for all. They quarreled bitterly. Both were young, both had bad tampers, and each saw his side as the right of the matter—"

"Regular Ralestones, weren't they?" commented Val slyly.

"Undoubtedly," agreed Rupert. "Well, at last Richard started for the house, his brother in pursuit.

"Then they fought, here in this very hall. And not with words this time, but with the rapiers Richard had brought back from France. A slave named Falesse, who had been the twins' childhood nurse was the only witness to the end of that duel. Richard lay face down across the hearthstone as she came screaming down the stairs."

Ricky was studying the gray stone.

"By rights," Val agreed with her unspoken thought, "there ought to be a stain there. Unfortunately for romance, there isn't."

"Rick was standing by the door," Rupert continued. "When Falesse reached his brother, he laughed unsteadily and half raised his sword in a duelist's salute. Then he was

27

gone. But there were two swords on the floor. And that niche was empty.

"When he fled into the night storm with his brother's blood staining his hands, Rich Ralestone took the Luck of his house with him.

"After almost a year of invalidism, Richard recovered. He never married his American beauty. But in 1819 he took a wife, a young Creole lady widowed by the Battle of New Orleans. Of Rick nothing was heard again, although his brother searched diligently for more than thirty years."

"How," Val grinned at his brother, "did Richard explain the little matter of the ghost which is supposed to walk at night?"

"I don't know. But when the Civil War broke out, Richard's son Miles was the master of Pirate's Haven. The once-great fortune of the family had shrunk. Business losses in the city, floods, a disaster at sea, had emptied the family purse—"

"The Luck getting in its dirty work by remote control," supplied the irrepressible Val.

"Perhaps. Young Miles had married in his teens, and the call to the Confederate colors brought both his twin sons under arms as well as their father.

"Miles, the father, fell in the First Battle of Bull Run. But Miles, the son and elder of the twins, a lieutenant of cavalry, came out of the war the only surviving male of his family.

"His brother Richard had been wounded and was home on sick leave when the Northerners occupied New Orleans. Betrayed by one of his former slaves, a mulatto who bore a grudge against the family, he was murdered by a gang of bullies and cutthroats who had followed the invading army.

"Richard had been warned of their raid and had managed to hide the family valuables in a secret place—somewhere within this very hall, according to tradition."

Val and Ricky sat up and looked about with wondering interest.

"But Richard was shot down in cold blood when he refused to reveal the hiding-place. His brother and some scouts, operating south without orders, arrived just in time to witness the last act. Miles Ralestone and his men summarily shot the murderers. But where Richard had so carefully concealed the last of the family treasure was never discovered.

"The war beggared the Ralestones. Miles went north in search of better luck, and this place was allowed to molder until it was leased in 1879 to a sugar baron. In 1895 it was turned over to a family distantly connected with ours. And since then it has been leased. We have had in all four tenants."

"But," Ricky broke in, "since the Luck went we have not prospered. And until it returns—"

Rupert tapped out his pipe against one of the fire irons. "It's nothing but a folk-tale," he told her.

"It isn't!" Ricky contradicted him vehemently. "And we've made a good beginning anyway. We've come back."

"If Rick took the Luck with him, I don't see how we have an earthly chance of finding it again," Val commented.

"It came back once before after it had gone from us,"

29

reminded his sister. "And I think that it will again. At least I'll hope so."

"Outside of the superstition, it would be well worth having. The names of the heads and heirs of the house are all engraved along the blade, from Sir Roderick on down. Seven hundred years of history scratched on steel." Rupert stretched and then glanced at his wrist-watch. "Ten to ten, and we've had a long day. Who's for bed?"

"I am, for one." Val swung his feet down from the couch, disturbing Satan who opened one yellow eye lazily.

Ricky stood by the fireplace fingering the wreath of stiff flowers carved in the stone. Val took her by the arm.

"No use wondering which one you push to reveal the treasure," he told her.

She looked up startled. "How did you know what I was thinking about?" she demanded.

"My lady, your thoughts, like little white birds—"

"Oh, go to bed, Val. When you get poetical I know you need sleep. Just the same," she hesitated with one foot on the first tread of the stair, "I wonder."

3

THE RALESTONES ENTERTAIN
AN UNOBTRUSIVE VISITOR

Val lay trapped in an underground cavern, chained to the floor. An unseen monster was creeping up his prostrate body. He could feel its hot breath on his cheek. With a mighty effort he broke his bonds and threw out his arms in an attempt to fight off his tormentor.

The morning sun was warm across his pillow, making him blink. On his chest stood Satan, kneading the bedclothes with his front paws and purring gently. From the open window came a fresh, rain-washed breeze.

Having aroused the sleeper, Satan deserted his post to hang half-way out the window, intent upon the housekeeping arrangements of several birds who had built in the hedges below. A moment later Val elbowed him aside to look out upon the morning.

It was a fine one. Wisps of mist from the bayou still hung about the lower garden, but the sun had already dried the brick-paved paths. A bee blundered past Val's nose, and he realized that it might be well to close the screen hanging shutter-like outside.

From the direction of the hidden water came the faint *putt-putt* of a motor-boat, but inside Pirate's Haven there was utter silence. As yet the rest of the family were not abroad. Val dropped his pajamas in a huddle by the bed and dressed leisurely, feeling very much at peace with this new world. Perhaps that was the last time he was to feel so for many days to come. He stole cautiously out of his room and tiptoed down halls and dark stairs, wanting to be alone while he discovered Pirate's Haven for himself.

The Long Hall looked chilly and bleak, even though patches of sunlight were fighting the usual gloom. On the hearthstone lay a scrap of white, doubtless Ricky's handkerchief. Val flung open the front door and stepped out on the terrace, drawing deep lungfuls of the morning air. The blossoms on the morning-glory vines which wreathed the edge of the terrace were open to the sun, and the birds sang in the bushes below. Satan streaked by and disappeared into the tangle. It was suddenly very good to be alive. The boy stretched luxuriously and started to explore, choosing the nearest of the crazy, wandering paths which began at the circle of the old carriage drive.

Here was evidence of last night's storm. Wisps of Spanish moss, torn from the great live-oaks of the avenue and looking like tufts of coarse gray horsehair, lay in water-logged mats here and there. And in the open places, the grass, beaten flat, was just beginning to rise again.

A rabbit scuttled across the path as it went down four steps of broken stone into a sort of glen. Here some early owner of the plantation had made an irregular pool of stone to be fed by the trickle of a tiny spring. Frogs the size of postage-stamps leaped panic-stricken for the water when Val's shadow fell across its rim. A leaden statue of the boy Pan danced joyously on a pedestal above. Ricky would love this, thought her brother as he dabbled his fingers in the chill water trying to catch the stem of the single lily bud.

Out of nowhere came a turtle to slide into the depths of the pool. The sun was very warm across Val's bowed shoulders. He liked the garden, liked the plantation, even liked the circumstances which had brought them there. Lazily he arose and turned.

By the steps down which he had come stood a slight figure in a faded flannel shirt and mud-streaked overalls. His bare brown feet gripped the stones as if to get purchase for instant flight.

"Hello," Val said questioningly.

The new-comer eyed young Ralestone warily and then his gaze shifted to the bushes beyond.

"I'm Val Ralestone." Val held out his hand. To his astonishment the stranger's mobile lips twisted in a snarl and he edged crabwise toward the bushes bordering the glen.

33

"Who are you?" Val demanded sharply.

"Ah has got as much right heah as yo' all," the boy answered angrily. And with that he turned and slipped into a path at the far end of the glen.

Aroused, Val hurried after him to reach the bayou levee. The quarry was already in midstream, wielding an efficient canoe paddle. On impulse Val shouted after him, but he never turned. A rifle lay across his knees and there were some rusty traps in the bottom of the flimsy canoe. Then Val remembered that Pirate's Haven lay upon the fringe of the muskrat swamps where Cajun and American squatters still carried on the fur trade of their ancestors.

But as Val stood speeding the departure of the uninvited guest, another canoe put off from the opposite shore of the bayou and came swinging across toward the rough wooden landing which served the plantation. A round brown face grinned up at Val as a powerful black clambered ashore.

"Yo' all up at de big house now?" he asked cheerily as he came up.

"If you mean the Ralestones, why, we got here last night," Val answered.

"You is Mistuh Ralestone, suh?" He took off his wide-brimmed straw hat and twisted it in his oversized hands.

"I'm Valerius Ralestone. My brother Rupert is the owner."

"Well, Mistuh Ralestone, suh, I'm de fahmah from 'cross water. Mistuh LeFleah, says yo'all is come to live heah agin. So mah woman, she says I should see if de fambly be heah yet and does want anythin'. Lucy, she's livin' heah, and her mammy and pappy, and her pappy's

mammy and pappy, has bin heah since befo' old Massa
Ralestone gone 'way. So Lucy, she jest nachely oneasy
'bout yo'all not gettin' things comfo'ble.''

"That is kind of her," Val answered heartily. "My
brother said something last night about wanting to see you
today, so if you'll come up to the house—''

"I be Sam, Mistuh Ralestone, suh. Work heah quite a
spell now."

"By the way," Val asked as they went up toward the
house, "did you see that boy in the canoe going downstream as you crossed? I found him in the garden and the
only answer he would give to my questions was that he
had as much right there as I had. Who is he?''

The wide smile faded from Sam's face. "Mistuh
Ralestone, suh, effen any no-'count trash comes 'round
heah agin, you bettah jest call de police. Nothin' but poah
white trash livin' down in de swamp places come to steal
whatevah dey lay han' on. Was dis boy big like you wi'
black hair an' a thin face?''

"Yes."

"Dat's de Jeems boy. He ain't got no kinfolk, lives jest
like a wil' man with a li'l huntin' an' a big lot stealin'. He
talk big. Say he belongs in de big house, not with swamp
folks. But jest pay no 'tenshun to him nohow.''

"Val! Val Ralestone! Where are you?" Ricky's voice
sounded clear through the morning air.

"Coming!" he shouted back.

"Well, make it snappy!" she shrilled. "The toast has
been burnt twice and—'' But what further catastrophe had
occurred her brother could not hear.

"You wants to git to de back do', Mistuh Ralestone? Dere's a sho't-cut 'cross here." Sam turned into a side path and Val followed.

Ricky was at the stove gingerly shifting a coffee-pot as her brother stepped into the kitchen. "Well," she snapped as he entered, "it's about time you were showing up. I've simply cracked my voice trying to call you, and Rupert's been talking about having the bayou dragged or something of the kind. Where have you been, anyway?"

"Getting acquainted with our neighbors. Ricky," he called her attention to the smiling face just outside the door, "this is Sam. He runs the home farm for us. And his wife is a descendant of the Ralestone house folks."

"Yassuh, dat's right. We's Ralestone folks, Miss 'Chanda. Mah Lucy sen' me to fin' out what yo'all is a-needin' done 'bout de place. She was in yisteday afo' yo'all come to do dustin' an' sich—"

"So that's why everything was so clean! That was nice of her—"

"Yo'all is Ralestones, Miss 'Chanda. An' Lucy say dat any Ralestones are a-goin' to fin' things jest ready when dey come." He beamed upon them proudly. "Lucy, she a-goin' be heah jest as soon as she gits de chillens set for de day. I come fust so's I kin see what Mistuh Ralestone done wan' done for rivah field."

"Where is Rupert?" Val broke in.

"Went out to see about the car. The storm last night wrecked the door of the carriage house—"

"That so?" Sam's eyes went round. "Den I bettah be a-gittin' out to see 'bout that. Scuse me, suh. 'Scuse me,

Miss 'Chanda.'' With a jerk of his head he left them. Val turned to Ricky.

"We seem to have fallen into good hands."

"It's my guess that his Lucy is a manager. He just does what she tells him to. I wonder how he knew my name?"

"LeFleur probably told them all about us."

"Isn't it odd—'' she turned off the gas, " 'Ralestone folks.' ''

"Loyalty to the Big House," her brother answered slowly. "I never thought that it really existed out of books."

"It makes me feel positively feudal. Val, I was born about a hundred years too late. I'd like to have been the mistress here when I could have ridden out in a victoria behind two matched bays, with a coachman and a footman up in front and my maid on the little seat facing me."

"And with a Dalmatian coach-hound running behind and at least three-fourths of the young bloods of the neighborhood as a mounted escort. I know. But those days are gone forever. Which leads me to another subject. What are we going to do today?"

"The dishes, for one thing," Ricky began ticking the items off on her fingers, "and then the beds. This afternoon Rupert wants us—that is, you and me—to drive to town and do some errands."

"Oh, yes, the list you two made out last night. Well, now that that's all settled, suppose we have some breakfast. Has Rupert been fed or is he thinking of going on a diet?"

"He'll be in—"

"Said she with perfect faith. All of which does not satisfy the pangs of hunger."

"Where's Lovey?"

"If you are using that sickening name to refer to Satan—he's out—hunting, probably. The last I saw of him he was shooting head first for a sort of bird apartment house over to the left of the front door. Here's Rupert. Now maybe we may eat."

"I've got something to tell you," hissed Ricky as the missing member of the clan banged the screen door behind him. Having so aroused Val's curiosity, she demurely went around the table to pour the coffee.

"How's the carriage house?" Val asked.

"Sam thinks he can fix it with some of that lumber piled out back of the old smoke-house." Rupert reached for a piece of toast. "What do you think of our family retainer?"

"Seems a good chap."

"LeFleur says one of the best. Possesses a spark of ambition and is really trying to make a go of the farm, which is more than most do around here. His wife, by all accounts, is a wonder. Used to be the cook-housekeeper here when the Rafaels had the place. LeFleur still talks about the two meals he ate here then. Sam tells me that she is planning to take us in hand."

"But we can't afford—" began Ricky.

"I gathered that money does not come into the question. The lady is rather strong-willed. So, Ricky," he laughed, "we'll leave you two to fight it out. But Lucy may be able to find us a laundress."

"Which reminds me," Ricky took a crumpled piece of white cloth from her pocket, "if this is yours, Rupert, you deserve to do your own washing. I don't know what you've got on it; looks like oil."

He took it from her and straightened out a handkerchief. "Not guilty this time. Ask little brother here." He passed over the dirty linen square. It was plain white—or it had been white before three large black splotches had colored it—without an initial or colored edge.

"I think he's prevaricating, Ricky," Val protested. "This isn't mine. I'm down to one thin dozen and those are the ones you gave me last Christmas. They have my initials on."

Ricky took back the disputed square. "That's funny. It certainly isn't mine. I'm sure one of you must be mistaken."

"Why?" asked Rupert.

"Because I found it on the hearth-stone in the hall this morning. It wasn't there last night or one of us would have seen it and picked it up, 'cause it was right there in plain sight."

"Sure it isn't yours, Val?"

He shook his head. "Positive."

"Queer," murmured Rupert and reached for it again. "It's a good quality of linen and it's almost new." He held it to his nose. "That's oil on it. But how—?"

"I wonder—" Val mused.

"What do you know?" asked Ricky.

"Well— Oh, it isn't possible. He wouldn't carry a handkerchief," her brother said half to himself.

"Who wouldn't?" asked Rupert. Then Val told them of his meeting with the boy Jeems and what Sam had had to say of him.

"Don't know whether I exactly like this." Rupert folded the mysterious square of stained linen. "As you say, Val, a boy like that would hardly carry a handkerchief. Also, you met him in the garden, while—"

"The person who left that was in this house last night!" finished Ricky. "And I don't like that!"

"The door was locked and bolted when I came down this morning," Val observed.

Rupert nodded. "Yes, I distinctly remember doing that before I went up to bed. But when I was going around the house this morning I discovered that there are French doors opening from the old ball-room to the terrace, and I didn't inspect their fastening last night."

"But who would want to come in here? There are no valuables left except furniture. And it would take three or four men and a truck to collect that. I don't see what he was after," puzzled Ricky.

Rupert arose from the table. "We have, it seems, a mystery on our hands. If you want to amuse yourselves, my children, here's the first clue. I've got to get back to the carriage house and my labors there."

He dropped the handkerchief on the table and left. Ricky reached for the "clue." "Awfully casual about it, isn't he?" she said. "Just the same, I believe that this is a clue and I know what our visitor was after, too," she finished triumphantly.

"What?"

"The treasure Richard Ralestone hid when the Yankee raiders came."

"Well, if our unknown visitor has as little in the way of clues as we have, he'll be a long time finding it."

"And we're going to beat him to it! It's somewhere in the Hall, and the secret—"

"See here," Val interrupted her, "what were you about to tell me when Rupert came in?"

She put the handkerchief in the breast pocket of her sport dress, buttoning the flap over it.

"Rupert's got a secret."

"What kind?"

"It has to do with those two brief-cases of his. You know, the ones he was so particular about all the way down here?"

Val nodded. Those bulging brief-cases had apparently contained the dearest of his roving brother's possessions, judging from the way Rupert had fussed if they were a second out of his sight.

"This morning when I came downstairs," Ricky continued, "he was sneaking them into that little side room off the dining-room corridor, the one which used to be the old plantation office. And when he came out and saw me standing there, he deliberately turned around and locked the door!"

"Whew!" Val commented.

"Yes, I felt that way too. So I simply asked him what he was doing and he made some silly remark about Bluebeard's chamber. He means to keep his old secret, too, 'cause he put the key on his keyring when he didn't know I was watching him."

"This is not the place for a rest cure," her brother

41

observed as he started to scrape and stack the dishes. "First someone unknown leaves his handkerchief for a calling card and then Rupert goes Fu Manchu on us. To say nothing of the rugged and unfriendly son of the soil whom I found bumping around the garden where he had no business to be."

"What was he like anyway?" asked his sister as she dipped soap flakes into the dish-water with a liberal hand.

"Oh, thin, and awfully brown. But not bad looking if it weren't for his mouth and that scowl of his. And he very distinctly doesn't like us. About my build, but quicker on his feet, tough looking. I wouldn't care to try to stop him doing anything he wanted to do."

"My dear, are you describing Clark Gable or someone you met in our garden this morning?" she demanded sweetly.

"Very well," Val retorted huffily into the depths of the oatmeal pan he was wiping, "you catch him next time."

"I will," was her serene answer as she wrung out the dish-cloth.

They went on to the upstairs work and Val received his first lesson in the art of bed-making under his sister's extremely critical tuition. It seemed that corners must be square and that dreadful things were likely to happen when wrinkles were not smoothed out. This exercise led them naturally to unpacking the remainder of the hand baggage and putting things away. It was after ten before Val came downstairs crab-fashion, wiping off each step behind him as he came with one of Ricky's three dust-cloths.

He paused on the landing to pull back the tapestry

curtain and open the windows above the alcove seat, letting in the freshness of the morning to rout some of the dank chill of the hall. Kneeling there, he watched Rupert come around the house. His brother had shed his coat and his sleeves were rolled up almost to his shoulders. There was a streak of black across his cheek and a large rip almost separated the collar from his shirt. Although he looked hot, cross, and tired, more like a day-laborer than a gentleman plantation owner whose ancestors had always "planted from the saddle," his stride had a certain buoyancy which it had lacked the day before.

With an idea of escaping Ricky by joining his brother, Val hurried downstairs and headed kitchenward. But his sister was there before him looking over a collection of knives of various lengths.

"Preparing for a little murder or two?" Val asked casually.

She jumped and dropped a paring knife.

"Val, don't do that! I wish you'd whistle or something while you're walking around in those tennis shoes. I can't hear you move. I'm looking for something to cut flowers with. There don't seem to be any scissors except mine and I'm not going to use those."

"Take that, Miss 'Chanda." A fat black hand motioned toward the paring knife.

Just within the kitchen door stood a wide, a very wide, black woman. Her neat print dress was stiff with starch from a recent washing, and round gold hoops swung proudly from her ears. Her black hair, straightened by main force of arm, had been set again in stiff, corrugated waves of

extreme fashion, but her broad placid face was both kind
and serene.

"I'm Lucy," she stated, thoroughly at her ease. "An'
this," she reached an arm behind her, pulling forth a girl
at least ten shades lighter and thirty-five shades thinner,
"is mah sistah's onliest gal-chil', Letty-Lou. Mak' yo'
mannahs, Letty. Does yo' wan' Miss 'Chanda to think yo'
is a know-nothin' from th' swamp?"

Thus sternly admonished, Letty-Lou ducked her head
shyly and murmured something in a die-away voice.

"Letty-Lou," announced her aunt, "has come to do fo'
yo'all, Miss 'Chanda. I learned her how to do fo' ladies.
She is good at scrubbin', cleanin' an such. I done train'd
her mahse'f."

Letty-Lou looked at the floor and twisted her thin hands
behind her back.

"But," protested Ricky, "we're not planning to have
anyone do for us, Lucy."

"That's all right, Miss 'Chanda. Yo's not gittin' a
know-nothin'. Letty-Lou, she knows her work. She kin
cook right good.'

"We can't take her," Val backed up Ricky. "You
must understand, Lucy, that we don't have much money
and we can't pay for—"

"Pay fo'!" Lucy's indignant sniff reduced him to his
extremely unimportant place. "We's not talkin' 'bout pay
workin', Mistuh Ralestone. Letty-Lou don' git no pay but
her eatments. 'Co'se, effen Miss 'Chanda wanna give her
some ole clo's now an' den, she kin tak' dem. Letty-Lou,
she don' hav' to git a pay-work job, her pappy make's a

good livin'. But Miss 'Chanda ain' a-goin' to tak' keer dis big hous' all by herself! We's Ralestone folks. Letty-Lou, git on youah ap'on an' git to work.''

"But we can't let her," Ricky raised her last protest.

"Miss 'Chanda, we's Ralestone folks. Mah gran' pappy Bob was own man to Massa Miles Ralestone. He fit in de wah 'longside o' Massa Miles. When de wah was done finish'd, the two of 'em come home togethah. Massa Miles call mah gran'pappy in an' say, 'Bob, yo'all is free an' I'se a ruinated man. Heah is fiv' dollahs gol' money, which is all I got left. Yo' kin hav' youah hoss.' An' Bob, he say, 'Cap'n Miles dese heah Yankees done said I'm free but nobody says I ain't a Ralestone man. What time does yo' wan' breakfas' in de mornin'?' Then when Massa Miles wen' no'th to make his fo'tune, he told Bob, 'Bob, I'se leavin' dis heah house in youah keer.' An', Miss 'Chanda, we done look aftah Pirate's Haven evah since, me gran'pappy, me pappy, Sam an' me.''

Ricky held out her hand. "I'm sorry, Lucy. You see, we don't understand very well, we've been away so long."

4

PISTOLS FOR TWO—COFFEE
FOR ONE

Val braced himself against the back of the convertible's seat and struggled to hold the car to a road which was hardly more than a cart track. Twice since Ricky and he had left Pirate's Haven they had narrowly escaped being bogged in the mud which had worked up through the thin crust of gravel on the surface.

To the south lay the old cypress swamps, dark glens of rotting wood and sprawling vines. A spur of this unsavory no-man's land ran close along the road, and looking into it one could almost believe, fancied Val, in the legends told by the early French explorers concerning the giant monsters who were supposed to haunt the swamps and wild lands at the mouth of the Mississippi. He would not have been surprised to see a brontosaurus peeking coyly down at him from twenty feet or so of neck. It was just the sort of place any self-respecting brontosaurus would have wallowed in.

But at last they won free from that place of cold and dank odors. Passing through Chalmette, they struck the main highway. From then on it was simple enough. St. Bernard Highway led into St. Claude Avenue and that melted into North Rampart street, one of the boundaries of the old French city.

"Can't we go slower?" complained Ricky. "I'd like to see some of the city without getting a crick in my neck from looking over my shoulder. Watch out for St. Anne Street. That's one corner of Beauregarde Square, the old Congo Square—"

"Where the slaves used to dance on Sundays before the war. I know; I've read just as many guide-books as you have. But there is such a thing as obstructing traffic. Also we have about a million and one things to do this afternoon. We can explore later. Here we are; Bienville Avenue. No, I will *not* stop so that you can see that antique store. Six blocks to the right," Val reminded himself.

"Val, that was the Absinthe House we just passed!"

"Yes? Well, it would have been better for a certain ancestor of ours if he had passed it, too. That was Jean Lafitte's headquarters at one time. Exchange Street—the next is ours."

They turned into Chartres Street and pulled up in the next block at the corner of Iberville. A four-story house coated with grayish plaster, its windows framed with faded green shutters and its door painted the same misty color, confronted them. There was a tiny shop on the first floor.

A weathered sign over the door announced that Bonfils et Cie. did business within, behind the streaked and bluish glass of the small curved window-panes. But what business Bonfils and Company conducted was left entirely to the imagination of the passer-by. Val locked the roadster and took from Ricky the long legal-looking envelope which Rupert had given them to deliver to Mr. LeFleur.

Ricky was staring in a puzzled manner at the shop when her brother took her by the arm. "Are you sure that you have the right place? This doesn't look like an office to me."

"We have to go around to the courtyard entrance. LeFleur occupies the second floor."

A small wooden door, reinforced with hinges of hand-wrought iron, opened before them, making them free of a courtyard paved with flagstones. In the center a tall tree shaded the flower bed at its foot and threw shadows upon the first of the steps leading to the upper floors. The Ralestones frankly stared about them. This was the first house of the French Quarter they had seen, although their name might have admitted them to several closely guarded Creole strongholds. LeFleur's house followed a pattern common to the old city. The lower floor fronting on the street was in use only as a shop or store-room. In the early days each shopkeeper lived above his place of business and rented the third and fourth floors to aristocrats in from their plantations for the fashionable season.

A long, narrow ell ran back from the main part of the house to form one side of the courtyard. The ground floor of this contained the old slave quarters and kitchens, while the second was cut into bedrooms which had housed the young men of the family so that they could come and go at will without disturbing the more sedate members of the household. These small rooms were now in use as the offices of Mr. LeFleur. From the balcony, running along the ell, onto which each room opened, one could look down into the courtyard. It was on this balcony that the lawyer met them with outstretched hands after they had given their names to his dark, languid young clerk.

"But this is good of you!" René LeFleur beamed on them impartially. He was a small, plumpish, round-faced man in his early forties, who spoke in perpetual italics. His eyebrows, arched over-generously by Nature, gave him a look of never-ending astonishment at the world and all its works. But his genial smile was kindness itself. Unaccustomed as Val was to sudden enthusiasms, he found himself liking René LeFleur almost before his hand gripped Val's.

"Miss Ralestone, it is a pleasure, a very great pleasure, to see you here! And this," he turned to Val, "this must be that brother Valerius both you and Mr. Ralestone spoke so much of during our meeting in New York. You have safely recovered from that most unfortunate accident, Mr. Ralestone? But of course, your presence here is my answer.

49

And how do you like Louisiana, Miss Ralestone?'' His eyes behind his gold-rimmed eyeglasses sparkled as he tilted his head a fraction toward Ricky as if to hear the clearer.

"Well enough. Though we've seen very little of it yet, Mr. LeFleur.''

"When you have seen Pirate's Haven,'' he replied, "you have seen much of Louisiana.''

"But we're forgetting our manners!'' exclaimed the girl. "We want to thank you for everything you've done for us. Rupert said to tell you that while he doesn't care for beans as a rule, the beans we found in our cupboard were very superior beans.''

Mr. LeFleur hooted with laughter like a small boy. "He is droll, is that brother of yours. And has Sam been to see you?''

"Sam and—Lucy,'' answered Ricky with emphasis. "Lucy has decided to take us in hand. She has installed Letty-Lou over our protests.''

The little lawyer nodded complacently. "Yes, Lucy will take care of you. She is a master housekeeper and cook—ah!'' His eyes rolled upward. "And Mr. Ralestone, how is he?''

"All right. He's going over the farm with Sam this afternoon. We were sent in his place to give you the papers he spoke to you about.''

At Ricky's answer, Val held out the envelope he had carried. To their joint surprise, LeFleur pounced upon it and withdrew to the window of the room into which he had conducted them. There he spread out the four sheets of yellowed paper which the envelope had contained.

"What were we carrying?" whispered Ricky. "Part of Rupert's deep, dark secret?"

"No," her brother hissed back, "those are the plans of the Patagonian fort which were stolen from the Russian Embassy last Thursday by the beautiful woman spy disguised with a long green beard. You know, the proper first chapter of an international espionage thriller. You are the dumb but beautiful newspaper reporter on the scent, and I—"

"The even dumber G-man who spends most of his time running three steps ahead of Fu Chew Chow and his gang of oriental demons. In the second chapter—"

But a glance at Mr. LeFleur's face as he turned away from the window put an end to their nonsense. Gone was his smile, his beaming good-will toward the world. He seemed a little tired, a trifle stooped. "Not here then," he said slowly to himself as he slipped the papers back into the envelope.

"Mr. Valerius," he looked up at the boy very seriously, "the LeFleurs have served the Ralestones, acting as their men of business, for over a hundred years. We owe your family a great debt. When young Denys LeFleur was shipped over here to New Orleans under false accusation of his enemies, the first Richard Ralestone became his patron. He helped the boy salvage something from the wreck of the LeFleur fortunes in France to start anew in a decent profession under tolerable surroundings, when others of his kind died miserably as beggars on the mud flats. Twice before have we been forced to be the bearers of ill news, but—'' he shrugged, ''that was in the past. This lies in the future.''

''What does?'' asked Ricky.

''It is such a tangle,'' he said, running his hand through his short, gray-streaked hair. ''A tangle such as lawyers are supposed to delight in. But they don't, I assure you that they don't, Miss Ralestone. Not if they have their client's interest at heart. You know, of course, of the missing Ralestone—Roderick?''

Ricky and Val both nodded. Mr. LeFleur spread out his plump hands in a queer little gesture as if he were pushing something away. ''This whole unfortunate business begins with him. As far as we know today, he and his brother were co-owners of Pirate's Haven. When young Roderick disappeared, he was still part owner. Although he was presumed dead, he was never lawfully declared so. Pirate's Haven was simply assumed to be the property of your branch of the family.''

''Our branch of the family?'' Val echoed him. ''Do you mean that some descendant of Roderick has appeared to put in a claim?''

''That is the problem. Three days ago a man came to my office. He said that he is the direct descendant of Roderick Ralestone and that he can produce proof of that fact.''

''And he wants his share of the estate?'' asked Ricky shrewdly.

''Yes.''

"He can keep on wanting," Val said shortly. "We've nothing to give."

"There's Pirate's Haven," pointed out Mr. LeFleur.

"But he can't—" Ricky's hand closed about her brother's wrist.

"Naturally he can't take it," Val assured her hotly. "Pirate's Haven is ours. This looks to me like blackmail. He'll threaten to stir up a lot of trouble unless we buy him off."

Mr. LeFleur nodded. "That is perhaps the motive behind it all."

"Well," Val forced a laugh, "then he loses. We haven't the money to buy him off."

"Neither have you the money to fight a case through the courts, Mr. Valerius," answered the lawyer soberly.

"But there is some chance, there must be!" urged Ricky.

"I submitted the full case to Mr. John Stanton yesterday—Mr. Stanton is our local authority on cases of this type. He has informed me that there is a single ray of hope. Frankly, I find this claimant a dubious person, but a shrewd one. He knows that he has the advantage now, but should we gain the upper hand, we could, I believe, rid ourselves of him. Our chance lies in the past. This was first a French and then a Spanish colony. Under both rules the law of primogeniture sometimes held force. That is, an estate passed to the eldest son of a family. Your estate was such a one. In fact, we possess in this very office old charters and papers which state that the property was entailed after the European custom. If that were so, the courts might declare that the elder of the twins born in 1788 was the sole owner of Pirate's Haven.

"But which of the twin brothers was the elder? You will say at once, Richard. But your rival will say Roderick. And there is no proof. For in the spring, two months after the birth of the boys, most of the family papers were destroyed in the great fire which almost wiped out the city and burned the Ralestone town house. There is no birth record in existence. I appealed to your brother to return to me these papers which Miles Ralestone took north with him after the war. You returned them today but there was nothing in them of any value to this case.

"However, if you can find such proof, that Richard Ralestone was the elder and thus the legal heir under the laws of Spain, then we shall have a solid fact upon which to base our fight."

"There is such a proof," began Ricky slowly.

"What? Where?" demanded Mr. LeFleur.

"Don't you remember, Val," she turned to him, "what Rupert said about the Luck last night—that the names of the heirs were engraved upon its blade? We'll have to find the Luck! We'll just have to!"

"But Roderick took the Luck with him. And if it's still in existence, this rival will have it now," her brother reminded her.

"Yes, of course, I was forgetting—" her voice trailed off into silence and Val stared at her with a dropped jaw. Such a quick change of manner was totally unlike Ricky. "Yes," she repeated slowly and distinctly, "I guess we're the losers—"

"For Pete's sake—" he began hotly and then he saw her hand making furious motions in his direction from behind the screen of her large purse. "Well, I suppose we are in a hole." He managed to mend his tone a fraction. "Rupert will probably be in to see you tomorrow, Mr. LeFleur."

"It would be well for him to become acquainted with the whole matter as quickly as possible," agreed the unhappy Creole. "You may tell Mr. Ralestone that I am, of course, having this claimant thoroughly investigated. We shall have to wait and see. Time is a big factor," he murmured as if to himself.

Ricky smiled brightly. There was a sort of eagerness about her, as if she were wild to be off. "Then we'll say good-bye for the present, Mr. LeFleur. And may I mention again how much we have appreciated your thoughtfulness?"

René LeFleur aroused himself. "But it was a pleasure, a very great pleasure, Miss Ralestone. You are returning to Pirate's Haven now?"

"Well—" she hesitated. Mystified at what lay behind her unexplainable actions, Val could only stand and listen. "We did have some errands. Of course, this news—"

LeFleur gestured widely. "But it will come all right. It must. There are papers somewhere."

Firmly Ricky broke away from more protracted farewells. As the Ralestones turned out of the courtyard into which their host had conducted them, Val matched his step with hers.

"Well? What's the matter?" he demanded.

"We had an eavesdropper."

Val stopped short. "What do you mean?"

"I was facing the door to the balcony. There was the shadow of a head on the floor. When you spoke about Rick having the sword, it went away—the shadow, I mean. But someone had been listening and now he knows about the Luck and what it means to us."

Aiming a kick at the nearest tire of the convertible, Val regarded the mud-stained rubber moodily. "Fine mess!"

"Yes, isn't it? And there seems to be no loose end to the thing," Ricky protested. "It's like holding a big tangle of wool and being told to have it all straightened out before night—the plot of a fairy-tale. We have so many odd sections but no ends. There's that boy in the garden this morning who said that he has as much right at Pirate's Haven as we have, and then there's that handkerchief, and now this man who claims half the estate—"

"And our mysterious listener," finished her brother. "What shall we do now? Go home?"

"No. We might as well do the errands." She seated herself in the car. "Val—"

"Yes?"

"I know one thing." She leaned toward him and her eyes shone green as they did when she was excited or greatly troubled. "We aren't going to let go of our tangle until we do find an end. We *are* the Ralestones of Pirate's Haven and we are going to continue to be the Ralestones of Pirate's Haven."

"In spite of the enemy? I agree." Val stepped on the starter. "You know, a hundred years ago there would have been a very simple remedy for this rival-claimant business."

"What?"

"Pistols for two—coffee for one. Rupert or I would have met him out at the dueling oaks and that would have been the end of him."

"Or you. But dueling—here!"

"Very common. The finest fencing masters on the North American continent plied their trade here. Why, one, Pepe Llula, the most famous duelist of his time, became the guardian of a cemetery just so, as gossip rumored, he could have some place to bury his opponents.

"Then on the other hand, if dueling were too risky, we might have had him voodooed, had we lived back in the good old days. Paid that voodoo queen—what was her name? Marie something or other—to put a curse on him so he'd just wither away."

"And serve him right, too." Ricky stared straight before her. "I don't know how you feel about it, but I'm not going to give up Pirate's Haven without a fight. It's—it's the first real home we've ever had. Rupert's older; he's spent his time traveling and seeing the world; it may not mean so much to him. But you and I, Val— You know what it's been like! Schools, and spending the holidays with aunts or in those frightful camps, never getting a chance to be together. We can't—we just can't have this only to lose it again. We can't!" her voice broke.

"So we won't."

"Val, when you say things like that, I can almost believe them. If—if we do lose, let's stick together this time. Promise?" her voice lifted in an effort toward lightness.

"I promise. After this it will be the two of us together. Do you know, I've never really had a chance to get acquainted with my very good-looking sister."

She laughed. "I can't very well curtsy while sitting down in here, but 'thank yuh for them purty words, stranger.' And now for the express station. Then you are to stop at the Southeastern News Association headquarters for something of Rupert's and—"

The afternoon went quickly enough. They despatched the rest of their possessions from the express station to Pirate's Haven, went on a round of miscellaneous shopping, picked up a weighty box at the News Association, and ended up at five o'clock by visiting that institution of New Orleans, a coffee-house. Ricky was earnestly peeking into one of her ten or so small bags. They had parked the car and Val complained that he had become a sort of packhorse, and anything but patient one.

"What if your feet do hurt," his sister said wearily as she closed the bag and reached for another. "So do mine. These sidewalks feel like red-hot iron. I'll bet I could do one of those fakir tricks where you're supposed to walk over red-hot plowshares."

"Not only my feet but also my backbone is protesting. Whether you have reached the end of that *Anthony Adverse* of a shopping list or not, we're going home! And what *are* you looking for? You've opened all those bags at least twice and dropped no less than three on the floor each time," he snapped irritably.

"My pralines. I'm sure I gave them to you to carry. I've

58

heard of New Orleans pralines all my life, so I got some today and now they've disappeared.

"They were probably included in that last armload of parcels I stowed in the car. Are you through?"

Ricky looked into her coffee-cup. "It's empty, so I guess I am. Where is the car? I'm so lost I don't know where we are now."

"We left it about three blocks away on the sunny side of the street," Val informed her with the relish of one who is thoroughly tired of his present existence. "If this is your usual behavior on a shopping trip, Rupert may bring you in the next time. Half an hour to choose a toothbrush-mug in the ten-cent store!"

"For a person who spends a good fifteen minutes matching a tie and a handkerchief," sniffed Ricky as she rose, "you're in a hurry to criticize others."

"Come *on!*" her brother almost howled as he scooped up the packages.

"Anyway, we won't have to get supper or wash the dishes or anything." She pulled off her hat as she settled herself in the car. "It's so beastly hot, but it'll be cooler at home. Do you suppose we could go swimming in the bayou?"

"I don't see why not." Val guided the roadster into a side street. "Where's that map of the city? We've got to see how to get back on to North Rampart from here."

"I'll look." Ricky bent her head and so she did not see the two figures walking close together and so rapt in conversation that the one on the curb side brushed against a lamp-post.

Now just what, considered Val, was the slim young clerk from Mr. LeFleur's office telling that red-faced man in the too-snug suit? He would have liked to have overheard a word or two. Perhaps he had become unduly suspicious but—he had his doubts.

"We turn left at the next corner," said Ricky.

Val changed gears and drove on.

5

THEIR TENANT DISCOVERS THE
RALESTONES

Val stood on the small ornamental bridge pitching twigs
down into the tiny garden brook. A moody frown creased
his forehead. Under his feet lay a pair of pruning-shears he
had borrowed from Sam with the intention of doing something about the jungle which surrounded Pirate's Haven on
three sides. That is, he had intended doing something, but
now—

"Penny for your thoughts."

"Lady," he answered dismally without turning around,
"you can have a bushel of them for less than that."

"There is a neat expression which describes you beautifully at this moment," commented Ricky as she came up beside her brother. "Have you ever heard of a 'sour puss'?"

"Several times. Oh, what's the use!" Val kicked at a long twig. A warm wind brought in its hold the heavy scent of flowering bushes and trees. His shirt clung to his shoulders damply. It was hot even in the shade of the oaks. Rupert had gone to town to see LeFleur and hear the worst, so that Pirate's Haven, save for themselves and Letty-Lou, was deserted.

"Come on," Ricky's arm slid through his, "let's explore. Think of it—we've been here two whole days and we don't know yet what our back yard looks like. Rupert says that our land runs clear down into the swamp. Let's go see."

"But I was going to—" He made a feeble beginning toward stooping for the pruning-shears.

"Val Ralestone, nobody can work outdoors in this heat, and you know it. Now come on. Bring those with you and we'll leave them in the carriage house as we pass it. You know," she continued as they went along the path, "the trouble with us is that we haven't enough to do. What we need is a good old-fashioned job."

"I thought we were going to be treasure hunters," he protested laughingly.

"That's merely a side-line. I'm talking about the real thing, something which will pay us cash money on Saturday nights or thereabout."

"Well, we can both use a typewriter fairly satisfactorily,"

Val offered. "But as you are the world's worst speller and I am apt to become entangled in my commas, I can't see us the shining lights of any efficient office. And while we've had expensive educations, we haven't had practical ones. So what do we do now?"

"We sit down and think of one thing we're really good at doing and then— Val, what is that?" She pointed dramatically at a mound of brick overgrown with vines. To their right and left stretched a row of tumble-down cabins, some with the roofs totally gone and the doors fallen from the hinges.

"The old plantation bake oven, I should say. This must be what's left of the slave quarters. But where's the carriage house?"

"It must be around the other side of the big house. Let's try that direction anyway. But I think you'd better go first and do some chopping. This dress may be a poor thing but it's my own and likely to be for some time to come. And short of doing a sort of snake act, I don't see how we're going to get through there."

Val applied the shears ruthlessly to vine and bush alike, glad to find something to attack. The weight of his depression was still upon him. It was all very well for Ricky to talk so lightly of getting a job, but talk would never put butter on their bread—if they could afford bread.

"You certainly have done a fine job of ruining that!"

Val surpassed Ricky's jump by a good inch. By the old bake oven stood a woman. A disreputable straw hat with a raveled brim was pulled down over her untidy honey-colored hair and she was rolling up the sleeves of a stained smock to bare round brown arms.

"It's very plain to the eye that you're no gardener," she continued pleasantly. "And may I ask who you are and what you are doing here? This place is not open to trespassers, you know."

"We did think we would explore," answered Ricky meekly. "You see, this all belongs to my brother." She swept her hand about in a wide circle.

"And just who is he?"

"Rupert Ralestone of Pirate's Haven."

"Good—!" Their questioner's hand flew to cover her mouth, and at the comic look of dismay which appeared on her face, Ricky's laugh sounded. A moment later the stranger joined in her mirth.

"And here I thought that I was being oh so helpful to an absent landlord," she chuckled. "And this brother of yours is *my* landlord!"

"How—? Why, we didn't know that."

"I've rented your old overseer's house and am using it for my studio. By the way, introductions are in order, I believe. I am Charity Biglow, from Boston as you might guess. Only beans and the Bunker Hill Monument are more Boston than the Biglows."

"I'm Richanda Ralestone and this is my brother Valerius."

Miss Biglow grinned cheerfully at Val. "That won't do, you know; too romantic by far. I once read a sword-and-cloak romance in which the hero answered to the name of Valerius."

"I haven't a cloak nor a sword and my friends generally call me Val, so I hope I'm acceptable," he grinned back at her.

"Indeed you are—both of you. And what are you doing now?"

"Trying to find a building known as the carriage house. I'm beginning to believe that its existence is wholly mythical," Val replied.

"It's over there, simply yards from the direction in which you're heading. But suppose you come and visit me instead. Really, as part landlords, you should be looking into the condition of your rentable property."

She turned briskly to the left down the lane on which were located the slave cabins and guided the Ralestones along a brick-paved path into a clearing where stood a small house of typical plantation style. The lower story was of stone with steep steps leading to a balcony which ran completely around the second floor of the house.

As they reached the balcony she pulled off her hat and threw it in the general direction of a cane settee. Without that wreck of a hat, with the curls of her long bob flowing free, she looked years younger.

"Make yourselves thoroughly at home. After all, this is your house, you know."

"But we didn't," protested Ricky. "Mr. LeFleur didn't tell us a thing about you."

"Perhaps he didn't know." Charity Biglow was pinning back her curls. "I rented from Harrison."

"Like the bathroom," Val murmured and looked up to

65

find them staring at him. "Oh, I just meant that you were another improvement that he had installed," he stammered. Miss Biglow nodded in a satisfied sort of way. "Spoken like a true southern gentleman, though I don't think in the old days that bathrooms would have crept into a compliment paid to a lady. Now I did have some lemonade—if you will excuse me," and she was gone into the house.

Ricky smiled. "I like our tenant," she said softly.

"You don't expect me to disagree with that, do you?" her brother had just time enough to ask before their hostess appeared again complete with tray, glasses, and a filled pitcher which gave forth the refreshing sound of clinking ice. And after her paraded an old friend of theirs, tail proudly erect. "There's our cat!" cried Ricky.

Val snapped his fingers. "Here, Satan."

After staring round-eyed at both of them, the cat crossed casually to the settee and proceeded to sharpen his claws.

"Well, I like that! After I shared my bed with the brute, even though I didn't know it until the next morning," Val exploded.

"Why, where did you meet Cinders?" asked Miss Biglow as she put down the tray.

"He came to us the first night we were at Pirate's Haven," explained Ricky. "I thought he was a ghost or something when he scratched at the back door."

"So that's where he was. He used to go over to the Harrisons' for meals a lot. When I'm working I don't keep very regular hours and he doesn't like to be neglected. Come here, Cinders, and make your manners."

Replying to her invitation with an insolent flirt of his tail, Cinders, whom Val continued obstinately to regard as "Satan," disappeared around the corner of the balcony. Charity Biglow looked at them solemnly. "So obedient," she observed; "just like a child."

"Are you an artist, too?" Ricky asked as she put down her glass.

Miss Biglow's face wrinkled into a grimace. "My critics say not. I manage to provide daily bread and sometimes a slice of cake by doing illustrations for action stories. And then once in a while I labor for the good of my soul and try to produce something my more charitable friends advise me to send to a show."

"May—may we see some of them—the pictures, I mean?" inquired Ricky timidly.

"If you can bear it. I use the side balcony for a workshop in this kind of weather. I'm working on a picture now, something more ambitious than I usually attempt in heat of this sort. But my model didn't show up this morning so I'm at a loose end."

She led them around the corner where Satan had disappeared and pointed to a table with a sketching board at one end, several canvases leaning face against the house, and an easel covered with a clean strip of linen. "My workshop. A trifle untidy, but then I am an untidy person. I'm expecting an order so I'm just whiling away my time working on an idea of my own until it comes."

Ricky touched the strip of covering across the canvas on the easel. "May I?" she asked.

"Yes. It might be a help, getting some other person's reaction to the thing. I had a clear idea of what I wanted to do when I started but I don't think it's turning out to be what I planned."

Ricky lifted off the cover. Val stared at the canvas.

"But that is he!" he exclaimed.

Charity Biglow turned to the boy. "And what do you mean—"

"That's the boy I saw in the garden, Ricky!"

"Is it?" She stared, fascinated, at the lean brown face, the untidy black hair, the bitter mouth, which their hostess had so skilfully caught in her unfinished drawing.

"So you've met Jeems." Miss Biglow looked at Val thoughtfully. "And what did you think of him?"

"It's rather—what did he think of me. He seemed to hate me. I don't know why. All I ever said to him was 'Hello.' "

"Jeems is a queer person—"

"Sam says that he is none too honest," observed Ricky, her attention still held by the picture.

Miss Biglow shook her head. "There is a sort of feud between the swamp people and the farmers around here. And neither side is wholly to be believed in their estimation of the other. Jeems isn't dishonest, and neither are a great many of the muskrat hunters. In the early days all kinds of outlaws and wanted men fled into the swamps and lived there with the hunters. One or two desperate men gave the whole of the swamp people a bad name and it has stuck. They are a strange folk back there in the fur country.

"Some are Cajuns, descendants of exiles from Evangeline's country; some are Creoles who took to that way of life after the Civil War ruined them. There's many a barefooted boy or girl of the swamps who bears a name that was once honored at the Court of France or Spain. And there are Americans of the old frontier stock who came down river with Andrew Jackson's army from the wilds of Tennessee and the Indian country. It's a strange mixture, and once in a while you find a person like Jeems. He speaks the uneducated jargon of his people but he reads and writes French and English perfectly. He has studied under Père Armand until he has a classical education such as was popular for Creole boys of good family some fifty years ago. Père Armand is an old man now, but he is as good an instructor as he is a priest.

"Jeems wants to make something of himself. He argues logically that the swamp has undeveloped resources which might save its inhabitants from the grinding poverty which is slowly destroying them. And it is Jeems' hope that he can discover some of the swamp secrets when he is fitted by training to do so."

"Who is he?" Val asked. "Is Jeems his first or last name?"

"His last. I have never heard his given name. He is very reticent about his past, though I do know that he is an orphan. But he is of Creole descent and he does have breeding as well as ambition. Unfortunately he had quite an unpleasant experience with a boy who was visiting the Harrisons last summer. The visitor accused Jeems of taking a fine rifle which was later discovered right where the boy had left it in his own canoe. Jeems has a certain pride and he was turned against all the plantation people. His attitude is unfortunate because he longs so for a different sort of life and yet has no contact with young people except those of the swamp. I think he is beginning to trust me, for he will come in the mornings to pose for my picture of the swamp hunter. Do you know,'' she hesitated, ''I think that you would find a real friend in Jeems if you could overcome his hatred of plantation people. You would gain as much as he from such an association. He can tell you things about the swamp—stories which go back to the old pirate days. Perhaps—''

Ricky looked up from the uncompleted picture. ''I think he'd be nice to know. But why does he look so—so sort of starved?''

''Probably because the bill of fare in a swamp cabin is not as varied as it might be,'' answered Charity Biglow. ''But you can't offer him anything, of course. I don't even know where he lives. And now, tell me about yourselves. Are you planning to live here?''

Her frank interest seemed perfectly natural. One simply couldn't resent Charity Biglow.

''Well,'' Ricky laughed ruefully, ''we can't very well live anywhere else. I think Rupert still has ten dollars—''

''After his expedition this morning, I would have my doubts of that,'' Val cut in. ''You see, Miss Biglow, we are back to the soil now.''

''Charity is the name,'' she corrected him. ''So you're down—''

70

"But not out!" Ricky hastened to assure her. "But we might be that." And then and there she told their tenant of the rival claimant.

Charity listened closely, absent-mindedly sucking the wooden shaft of one of her brushes. When Ricky had done, she nodded.

"Nice mess you've dropped into. But I think that your lawyer has the right idea. This is a neat piece of blackmail and your claimant will disappear into thin air if you have a few concrete facts to face him down with. Are you sure you've looked through all the family papers? No hiding-places or safes—"

"One," said Ricky calmly, "but we don't know where that is. In the Civil War days, after General Butler took over New Orleans, some family possessions were hidden somewhere in the Long Hall, but we don't know where. The secret was lost when Richard Ralestone was shot by Yankee raiders."

"Is he the ghost?" asked Charity.

"No. You ask that as if you know something," Val observed.

"Nothing but talk. There have been lights seen, white ones. And a while back my maid Rose left because she saw something in the garden one night."

"Jeems, probably," the boy commented. "He seems to like the place."

"No, not Jeems. He was sitting right on that railing when we both heard Rose scream."

"Val, the handkerchief!" Rick's hand arose to her but-

71

toned pocket. "Then there *was* someone inside the house that night. But why—unless they were after the treasure!"

"The quickest way to find out," her brother got up from the edge of the table where he had perched, "is to go and do a little probing of our own. We have a good two hours until lunch. Will you join us?" he asked Charity.

"You tempt me, but I've got to get in as much work on this as I can," she indicated her canvas. "And Jeems may show up even if it is late. So my conscience says 'No.' Unfortunately I do possess a regular rock-ribbed New England conscience."

"Rupert will be back by four," said Ricky. "Will your conscience let you come over for coffee with us then? You see how quickly we have adopted the native customs— coffee at four."

"Ricky," her brother explained, "desires to become that figure of Romance—the southern belle."

"Then we must do what we can to help her create the proper atmosphere," urged Charity solemnly.

"Even to the victoria and the coach-hound?" Val demanded in dismay.

"Well, perhaps not that far," she laughed. "Anyway, I accept your kind invitation with pleasure. I shall be there at four—if I can find a presentable dress. Now clear out, you two, and see what secrets of the past you can uncover before lunch time."

But their explorations resulted in nothing except slightly frayed tempers. Val had sounded what paneling there was, but as he had no idea what a hollow panel should sound like if rapped, he inwardly decided that he was not exactly fitted for such investigations.

Ricky broke two fingernails pressing the carving about the fireplace and sat down on the couch to state in no uncertain terms what she thought of the house, and of their ancestor who had been so misguided as to get himself shot after hiding the stuff. She ended with a brilliant but short description of Val's present habits and vices—which she added because he happened to have said, meekly enough, that if she would only trim her nails to a reasonable length, such accidents could be avoided.

When she had done, her brother sat back on the lowest step of the stairs and wiped his hands on his handkerchief.

"Seeing that I have been crawling about on my hands and knees inspecting cracks in the floor, I think I have as much right to lose my temper as you have. Short of tearing the house down, I don't see how we are going to find anything without directions. And I am *not* in favor of taking such a drastic step as yet."

"It's around here somewhere, I know it!" She kicked petulantly at the hearth-stone.

"That statement is certainly a big help," Val commented. "Several yards across and I don't know how many up and down—and you just know it's there somewhere. Well, you can keep on pressing until you wear your fingers out, but I'm calling it a day right now."

She did not answer, and he got stiffly to his feet. He was hot and more tired than he had been since he had left the hospital. Because he was just as sure as Ricky that the key to their riddle must be directly before them at that moment, he was thoroughly disgusted.

A strange sound from his sister brought him around. Ricky was not pretty when she cried. No pearly drops slipped down white cheeks. Her nose shone red and she sniffed. But Ricky did not cry often. Only when she was discouraged, or when she was really hurt.

"Why, Ricky—" Val began uncertainly.

"Go 'way," she hiccupped. "You don't care—you don't care 'bout anything. If we have to lose this—"

"We won't! We'll find a way!" he assured her hurriedly. "I'm sorry I snapped at you. I'm just tired and hot, and so are you. Let's go upstairs and freshen up. Lunch will be ready—"

"I kno-o-ow—" her sob deepened into a wail. "Then Rupert will laugh at us and—"

"Ricky! For goodness sake, pull yourself together!"

She looked up at him, round-mouthed in surprise at his sharpness. And then to his amazement she began to giggle, her giggles mixed with her sobs. "You do look so funny," she gasped, "like the stern father of a family. Why don't you fight back always when I get mean, Val?"

He grinned back at her. "I don't know. Shall I, next time?"

She rubbed her face with a businesslike air and tucked her handkerchief away. "There isn't going to be any next time," she announced briskly. "If there is—well—"

"Yes?" Val prompted.

"Then you can just spank me or something drastic.

Come on, I must look a sight. And goodness knows, you're no beauty with that black mark across your chin and your slacks all grimy at the knees. We've got to clean up before lunch or Letty-Lou will think we're some sort of heathen.''

With that she turned and led the way upstairs, totally recovered and herself again in spite of a red nose and suspiciously moist eyelashes.

6

SATAN GOES A-HUNTING AND
FINDS WORK FOR IDLE HANDS

"Val, did that cat go upstairs?" Ricky stood at the foot of the hall staircase frowning crossly. "If he did, you'll just have to go up and get him. I will not have him walking on the beds with muddy feet. There's enough to do here without cleaning up after a lazy cat. Where's Rupert?"

Her brother put aside his note-book and got up from the couch with a lazy stretch. Ricky's early-morning energy was apt to be a little irksome and Val had not had a good night. When one lies and stares up at a ceiling, one sometimes hears strange noises which cannot be accounted for by wind or creaking boards.

"He retired into Bluebeard's den right after breakfast and he hasn't appeared since."

"I should think that after what he heard yesterday he'd be doing something," she protested.

"And what is there for him to do? You know just how far we got with our investigations yesterday. Go rap on his door if you like and stir him up. But I don't think his welcome will be a cordial one."

Ricky sat down on the bottom step and pushed the hair back from her forehead. Suddenly she looked very small and faintly forlorn with all that expanse of age-blackened wood behind her.

"I can't understand you two at all. One would think you would be just as well pleased if our rival walked off with this place. You aren't even trying to fight!"

"Listen, Ricky, how can we fight when we have nothing solid to fight with? LeFleur is doing all he can, we have explored every possibility here—"

"Val, don't you *want* to stay here?" she interrupted him.

He looked around at stone and wood. Did he really want to? His instant hot anger at the thought of another owner there was his answer. Why, this house was a part of them, as much as if they had laid its foundation stones with their own hands. They had been brought up on its blood-stained legends, and on the one or two happier tales which had been lived within its walls. If they had to leave, they would regret it all their lives. And yet—Rupert seemed to take no interest in the claims of the rival, and only Ricky wanted to fight.

77

Ricky got up from the stairs.

"We might as well go up and catch that cat," she said.

At the top of the stairs Satan sat, his eyes upon the landing windows. Val reached out his hands for him, but in that single instant Satan was gone. A black tail disappeared around the door of the Jackson room.

"Oh, dear, I hope he isn't going to get on that bed." Ricky opened the door wider. "No, there he goes under instead of on it. Can you see him, Val?"

Her brother crouched and lifted the edge of the brocaded cover which swept to the floor. To Val's surprise a thin line of light showed along the wall at the head of the bed.

"Ricky, look behind the head of the bed! Is it fast against the wall?"

She started to the tall canopied head and pulled the faded fabrics away from the paneling. "No, there's about two feet here at the bottom. It doesn't show because the canopy covers it. And, Val, there's an opening here! Satan's trying to get through!"

"We need a flashlight."

"I'll get Rupert's. Val, promise not to go in—if it *is* a door—until I come back!"

"Of course; but hurry."

The flashlight revealed a wide panel which slid upward. Time and damp had warped the wood so that it no longer fitted snugly to the floor as the builder had intended. But the same warping made the door defy their efforts to raise it any higher. At last, by prying and pounding, they got it up perhaps a yard from the floor. Satan slipped through and they followed on hands and knees.

They crawled into a small room lighted by two round windows set like eyes in the wide wall. More than three-quarters of the space was filled with furniture and boxes wrapped in tarred canvas. The choking dust and general mustiness of the long-closed apartment drove Val to investigate the window fastenings and throw them open to the morning air.

"There must be another door somewhere," he said, calling Ricky away from a box where she was picking at the knotted rope which bound it. "All these things couldn't have been brought through that hole behind the bed."

"Here it is," she said a moment later, pointing to an oblong set flush with the wall. "It's bolted on this side."

"Let me open it and see where we are." Val fumbled at the rusty latch, but he had to use an iron poker from a discarded fire stand in the corner before he could hammer it back. Again the door resisted their efforts to push it open until Val flung his full weight against it. With a snapping report it swung open and he sprawled forward into the short hall which had once led into the garden wing, an ell of the house destroyed by roving British raiders during the days of 1815. The only wholly wooden portion of the house, it had been burnt and never rebuilt.

"Come on," Ricky pulled at Val's sleeve, "let's explore."

He looked at his black hands. "I would suggest some soap and water, several brooms, and some dusting cloths if we're going to do it right. Better make a regular house-cleaning party of it."

"Goodness, what have I strayed into?" Charity Biglow

79

stood in the lower hall staring at the younger Ralestones as they came through from the kitchen. They had both changed into their oldest and least respectable clothes. Ricky, in fact, was wearing a pair of Val's slacks and one of Rupert's shirts, and they were burdened with a broom which was long past its youth, several smaller brushes, and a great bundle of floor-cloths.

"We've found a secret room—" began Ricky.

"As one door has been in plain sight since the building of this house, it could hardly be called a secret room," Val objected.

"Well, we didn't know it was there until Satan found the back entrance for us. And now we're going to clean it out. It's full of furniture and boxes and things."

"Don't!" Charity held up a paint-streaked hand. "You will have me drooling in a moment. I don't suppose you could use another assistant? After all, it was my cat who found it for you. If you can provide me with a set of those weird coverings which seem to be your house-cleaning uniforms, I would just love to wield a broom in your company."

"The more the merrier," laughed Ricky. "I think Val has another pair of slacks—"

"That's right, dispose of my wardrobe before my face," he commented, balancing his load more carefully in preparation for climbing the stairs. "Only spare my white flannels, please. I'm saving those for the occasion when I can play the country gentleman in style."

Upstairs he braced open the hall door of the storage-room. The open windows had cleared the air within but they were too high and too small to admit enough light to reach the far corners. It would be best, they decided, to carry each box and piece of furniture to the hall for examination. With the zeal of treasure hunters they set to work.

Some time later, when Val was coaxing the second box through the door, they were interrupted.

"And just what is going on here?" Rupert stood at the end of the hall.

"Oh," Ricky smiled sweetly, "did we really disturb you?"

"Well, I did think that there was a troop of elephants doing tap dancing up here. But that isn't the point—just *what* are you doing?"

"Cleaning house." Ricky flicked a gray rag in his direction freeing a cloud of dust. "Don't you think it needs it?"

Rupert sneezed. "It seems so. But why—? Miss Biglow!"

Charity, extremely dirty—she had apparently run dusty hands across her forehead several times—had come to the door of the storage-room. At the sight of Rupert she flushed and made a hurried attempt at smoothing her hair.

"I—" she began, when Ricky interrupted her.

"Charity is helping us, which is more than we can say of you. Go back to your old den and hibernate. And then you can't look down that long nose of yours when we turn up the papers that'll save us from the poorhouse."

"That's telling him," Val murmured approvingly as he fanned himself with one of the cleaner cloths. "But perhaps we had better explain. You see, Satan went hunting

81

and found work for idle hands," and he told the tale of the sliding panel behind the bed.

When he had finished, Rupert laughed. "So you are still determined on treasure hunting, are you? Well, if it will keep you out of mischief, go to it."

"Rupert," Ricky faced him squarely, "don't be utterly insufferable. If you had one drop of hot blood in you, you'd be just as thrilled as we are. Just because you've been around and around the world until you got dizzy or something, you needn't stand there with that 'See-the-little-children-play' smirk on your face. You don't really care whether we lose Pirate's Haven or not, do you?"

Rupert straightened and the color crept up across his high cheek-bones. His mouth opened and then he closed it again without speaking the words he had intended, closed with a firmness which tightened his lips into a straight line.

"Don't stand there and glower at me," Ricky went on. "Why don't you say what you were going to? I'm just about tired of this world-weary attitude—"

"Ricky!" Val clapped his black hand over her mouth and turned to Charity. "Please excuse the fireworks. They are not usual, I assure you."

"Let me go!" Ricky twisted out of his grip. "I don't care if Charity does hear. She ought to know what we're really like!"

"Speak for yourself, my pet." The red had faded from Rupert's face. "You do have a nice little habit of speaking your mind, don't you? But on this occasion I believe you're at least eight-tenths right. I have been neglecting my opportunities. Suppose you let me get at that box, Val. And look here, if you are going to unpack these, why not move them down to the end of the hall and turn them out on a sheet?''

Charity and Ricky suddenly disappeared back into the room and were very busy whenever Rupert crossed their line of vision, but Val was heartily glad of his brother's help in lifting and pulling.

''Better not try to take this bedstead and stuff out,'' Rupert advised when they had the three boxes out in the hall. ''We have no need for it now, anyway.''

''I believe—yes, it is! A real Sergnoret piece!'' Charity was industriously rubbing away at the head of the bed. Rupert knelt down beside her.

''And just what is a Sergnoret piece?''

''A collector's item nowadays. François Sergnoret was one of the greatest cabinet-makers of New Orleans. See that 'S'—that's the way he always signed his work.''

''Treasure trove!'' cried Ricky. ''I wonder how much it's worth?''

''Exactly nothing to us.'' Rupert was running his hands across the mahogany. ''We couldn't sell anything from this house until the title is cleared.''

As Val moved around to the opposite side to see better, his foot struck against something on the floor. He stooped and picked up a box with a slanting cover, the whole black and smooth with age and the rubbing of countless hands.

''What's this?'' He had crossed to the door and was examining his find in the light.

Rupert's hand fell upon his shoulder. ''Val, be careful

of that. Charity, he's got something here!" He pulled her up beside him, not noting in his excitement that he had broken out of the formal shell which seemed to wall him in whenever she was around.

"A Bible box! And an authentic one, too!" She drew her fingers down the slope of the lid.

"And just what is it?" Val asked for the second time.

"These boxes were used in the seventeenth century for writing-desks and later to keep the large family Bibles in. But this is the first one I've ever seen outside of a museum. What's this on the lid?" She traced a worn outline. Val studied the design.

"Why, it's Joe! You know, that grinning skull we have stuck up all over the place to bolster up our superiority complex. That proves that this is ours, all right."

"Perhaps—" Ricky's eyes were round with excitement, "perhaps it belonged to Pirate Dick himself!"

"Perhaps it did," her younger brother agreed.

"Lift the lid." She was almost hopping on one foot in her impatience. "Let's see what's inside."

"No gold or jewels, I'll wager. How do you get the thing undone?"

"Here, let me try." Rupert took it from Val's hands and put it down on one of the chests, squatting on the floor before it. With the smallest blade of his penknife he delicately probed the fastening sunken in the wood.

"I could do a faster job," he remarked, "if you didn't all breathe down the back of my neck." They retreated two inches or so and waited impatiently. With a satisfied grunt he dropped his knife and pulled the lid up.

"Why, there's nothing it it!" Ricky's cry of disappointment was almost a wail.

"Nothing but that old torn lining." Val was as disgusted as she.

Rupert closed it again. "I'll rub this up some and put in another lining. This is too good a piece to hide away up here," and he put it carefully aside at the end of the hall.

Their investigations yielded nothing more except great quantities of dust, a mummified rat which even Satan refused to sniff at, and a large collection of spider webs. Having swept out the room, they went to wash their hands before unpacking the well-wrapped boxes.

When their swathing canvas and sacking was thrown aside, the boxes stood revealed as stout chests banded with iron. Charity paused before one. "This is a marriage chest, late seventeenth century, I would judge. Look there, under that carved leaf—isn't that a date?"

"Sixteen hundred ninety-three," Rupert deciphered. "That crest above it looks familiar. I know, it belonged to that French lady who married our pirate ancestor."

"The first Lady Richanda!" Ricky touched the chest lovingly. "Then this is mine, Rupert. Can't it be mine?" she coaxed.

"Of course. But it's locked, and as we don't have any keys which would fit the lock, you'll have to wait until we can get a locksmith out to work on it before you will know what's inside."

"I don't care. No," she corrected herself, "that's wrong; I do care. But anyway its mine!" She caressed the stiff carving with her fingers.

"What's this one?" Val turned to the second box. It, too, was fashioned of wood, but it was plain where the other was carved, and the iron bands across it were pitted with rust.

"A sea chest, I would say." Rupert touched the top gingerly. "By the feel, it's locked too. And I don't care to play around with it. The men who made things like these were too fond of having little poisoned fangs run into your hand when you tried to force the chest without knowing the trick. We'll have to leave this for an expert, too."

"What about the third?"

Charity laughed. "After your two treasures I'm afraid that this will be a disappointment." She indicated a small humpbacked trunk covered with moth-eaten horsehair. "No romance here. But the key is tied to the clasp beside the lock."

"Then open it before I expire of pure unsatisfied curiosity," Ricky begged. "Go on, Rupert. Hurry."

"Oh," she said a moment later, "it's full of nothing but a lot of books."

"What did you expect," Val asked her, "a skeleton? Do you know, I think that Rick's ghost, or whatever influence presides over this house, has a sense of humor. You find a room, or a trunk, or something which makes you feel that you are on the verge of getting what you want, and then it all fades into just nothing again. Now, by rights, that writing-desk should have contained the secret message which would have told us where to find a hidden passage or something. But what is in it? A couple of pieces of lining almost completely torn from the bottom.

I'll wager that when you open those chests you'll find nothing but a brick or 'April Fool' scrawled across the inside. This isn't true to any fiction I ever read," he ended plaintively.

"Good Heavens!" Charity was staring down at what lay within a portfolio she had opened.

"Don't tell me you have really found something!" Val exclaimed.

"It can't be true!" She still stared at what she held.

Ricky looked over her shoulder. "Why, it's nothing but a picture of a bird," she observed.

"It's a genuine Audubon," Charity corrected her.

"What!" With little regard for manners, Rupert snatched the portfolio from her hands. "Are you sure?"

"Yes. But you must take it in to the museum and get an expert opinion. It's wonderful!"

"Here's another." Reverently Rupert raised the first sketch and then the second. "Three, four, five, six," he counted.

"Was Audubon ever here?" Charity looked about the hall, a sort of awe coloring her voice.

"He might easily have been when he lived in New Orleans. Though we have no record of it," answered Rupert. "But these," he closed the portfolio carefully and knotted its strings, "speak for themselves. I'll take them to LeFleur tomorrow. We can't allow them to lie about here."

"I should hope not!" Charity eyed the portfolio wistfully. "Imagine actually owning six of those—"

"They won't pay our bills," said Ricky, practical for once in her life. Treasure to Ricky was not half a dozen sketches on yellowed paper but good old-fashioned gold with a few jewels thrown in for her own private satisfaction. The portfolio and its contents left her unmoved. Val admitted to himself that he, too, was disappointed. After all—well, treasure should be treasure.

Rupert carried the portfolio into his bedroom and locked it in one of his mysterious brief-cases which had somehow found its way upstairs.

The two chests they moved out farther into the hall and the trunk was placed back against the wall, ready for further investigation.

"Mistuh Ralestone," Letty-Lou, standing half-way up the back stairs, addressed Rupert, "lunch on de table. Effen yo'all doan come now, eatments will be spoiled."

"All right," he answered.

"Letty-Lou," called Ricky, "put on another plate. Miss Charity is staying to lunch."

"Miss 'Chanda, I done done it already. Yo'all comin' now?"

"You see how we are bullied," Ricky appealed to Charity. "Of course you're going to stay," she swept aside the other's protests. "What's food for, if not to feed your friends? Val, go wash up; your hands are frightful. I don't care if you did wash once; go and—"

"This is her little-mother-of-the-family mood," her younger brother explained to Charity. "It wears off after a while if you just don't notice it. But I will wash though," he looked at his hands, "I seem to need it."

"And don't use the guest towels," Ricky called after him. "You know that they're only to look at."

When Val emerged from the bathroom he found the hall deserted. Sounds from below suggested that his family had basely left him for food. He started along the passage. Not far from the stairs was the writing-desk where Rupert had left it. Val picked it up, thinking that he might as well take it along down with him.

7

BY OUR LUCK!

Depositing the desk on the seat of one of the hall chairs, Val started toward the dining-room, a grim hole which Lucy had calmly forced the family to use but which they all cordially disliked. Its paneled walls, crystal-hung chandelier, marble-fronted fireplace, and inlaid floor gave it the appearance of one of the less cozy rooms in a small palace. There were also two tasteful portraits of dead ducks which had been added as a finishing touch by some tenant during the eighties and which still remained upon the walls to Ricky's unholy joy.

But the long table, the high-backed chairs, the side

serving-table, and the two tall cabinets of china were fine enough pieces if one cared for the massive. Ricky's table-cloth of violent-hued peasant linen was not in keeping with the china and glassware Letty-Lou had set out upon it. Charity was commenting upon this ensemble as Val entered.

"Doesn't this red and green plaid seem a bit—well, bright?" The corners of her mouth twitched betrayingly.

"No," Ricky returned firmly. "This cloth matches the ducks."

"Oh, yes, the ducks," Charity eyed them. "So you consider that the ducks are the note you wish to emphasize?"

"Certainly." Ricky surveyed the picture hanging opposite her. "I consider them unique. Not everyone can have ducks in the dining-room nowadays."

"For which they should be eternally thankful," observed Rupert. "They are rather gaudy, aren't they?"

"Oh, but I like the expression in this one's glassy eye," Ricky pointed out. "You might call this study 'Gone But Not Forgotten.' "

"Corn-bread, please," Val asked, thus attempting to put an end to the art-appreciation class.

"I think," continued Ricky, undisturbed as she passed him the plate heaped with golden squares, "that they are slightly surrealist. They distinctly resemble the sort of things one is often pursued by in one's brighter nightmares."

"Do you have any really good pictures?" asked Charity, resolutely averting her gaze from the ducks.

"Three, but they've been loaned to the museum," answered Rupert. "Not by well-known painters, but they're historically interesting. There's one of the first Lady

Richanda, and one of the missing Rick. That's the best of the lot, according to LeFleur. I saw a photograph of it once. Come to think about it, Val looks a lot like the boy in the picture. He might have sat for it.''

They all turned to eye Val. He arose and bowed. ''I find these compliments too overwhelming,'' he murmured.

Rupert grinned. ''And how do you know that that remark was intended as a compliment?''

''Naturally I assumed so,'' his brother retorted with a dignity which disappeared as the piece of corn-bread in his hand broke in two, the larger and more liberally buttered portion falling butter side down on the table. Ricky smiled in a pained sort of way as she attempted to judge from her side of the table just how much damage Val's awkwardness had done.

''If you were the graceful hostess,'' he informed her severely, ''you would now throw your piece in the middle to show that anyone could suffer a like mishap.''

Ricky changed the subject hurriedly by passing beans to Charity.

''So Val looks like the ghost,'' Charity said a moment later. ''Now I will have to go to town and see that portrait. Just where is it?''

Rupert shook his head. ''I don't know. But it's listed in the catalogue as 'Portrait of Roderick Ralestone, Aged Eighteen.' ''

''Just Val's age, then.'' Ricky spooned some watermelon pickles onto her plate. ''But he was older than that when he left here.''

''Let's see. He was born in February, 1788, which

would make him fourteen when his parents died in 1802. Then he disappeared in 1814, twelve years later. Just twenty-six when he went," computed Rupert.

"A year younger than you are now," observed Ricky.

"And nine years older than yourself at this present date," Val added pleasantly. "Why this sudden interest in mathematics?"

"Oh, I don't know. Only somehow I always thought Rick was younger when he went away. I've always felt sorry for him. Wonder what happened to him afterwards?"

"According to our rival," Rupert pulled his coffee-cup before him as Letty-Lou took away their plates, "he just went quietly away, married, lived soberly, and brought up a son, who in turn fathered a son, and so on to the present day. A tame enough ending for our wild privateersman."

"I'll bet it isn't true. Rick wouldn't end like that. He probably went off down south and got mixed up in some of the revolutions they were having at the time," suggested Ricky. "He couldn't just settle down and die in bed. I could imagine him scuttling a ship but not being a quiet business man."

"He was one of Lafitte's men, wasn't he?" asked Charity. At their answering nods, she went on: "Lafitte was a business man, you know. Oh, I don't mean that forge he ran in town, but his establishment at Grande Terre. He was more smuggler than pirate, that's why he lasted so long. Even the most respected tradesmen had dealings with him. Why, he used to post notices right in town when he held auctions at Barataria, listing what he had to sell, mostly smuggled blacks and a few cargoes of luxuries from

Europe. He was a privateer under the rules of war, but he was never a real pirate. At least, that's the belief held nowadays.''

''We can't turn up our noses at pirates,'' laughed Ricky. ''This house was built by pirate gold. We only wish—''

From the hall came a dull thump. Ricky's napkin dropped from her hand into her coffee-cup. Rupert laid down his spoon deliberately enough, but there was a certain tension in his movements. Val felt a sudden chill. For Letty-Lou was in the kitchen, the family were in the dining-room. There should be no one in the hall.

Rupert pushed back his chair. But Val was already half-way to the door when his brother joined him. And Ricky, suddenly sober, was at their heels.

Zzzzzrupp! The slitting sound was clear as they burst into the hall. On the fur rug by the couch lay the writing-desk. Its lid was thrown back and by it crouched Satan industriously ripping the remnants of lining from its interior. As Rupert came up, the cat drew back, his ears flattened and his lips a-snarl.

''Cinders! What has he done?'' demanded Charity, swooping down upon her pet. At her coming, he fled under the couch out of reach.

Rupert picked up the desk. ''Nothing much,'' he laughed. ''Just torn all that lining loose, as I had planned to do.''

''What is this?'' Ricky disentangled a small slip of white from the torn and musty velvet. ''Why, it's a piece of paper,'' she answered her own question. ''It must have been under the lining and Satan pulled it out with the cloth.''

"Here," Rupert took it from her, "let me see it."

He scanned the faded lines of writing. "Val! Ricky!" He looked up, his face flushed with excitement. "Listen!"

"Gatty has returned from the city. The raiders calling themselves the 'Buck Boys' are headed this way. Gatty tells me that Alexander is with them, having deserted the plantation a week ago. Since his malice towards us is well known, it is easy to believe that he means us open harm. I am making my preparations accordingly. The valuables now under this roof, together with the proceeds from the last voyage of the blockade runner, *Red Bird,* I am putting in that safe place discovered by me in childhood, of which I have sometimes spoken. Remember the hint I once gave you—By Our Luck. Having written this in haste, I shall intrust it to Gatty—"

"That's the end; the rest is gone." Rupert stared down at the scrap of paper in his hand as if he simply could not believe in its reality.

"Richard wrote that." Ricky touched the note in awe. "But why didn't Gatty give it to Miles when he came?"

"Gatty was probably a slave who ran when the raiders appeared," suggested Rupert. "He or she must have hidden this in here before leaving. We'll never know."

"But we've got our clue!" cried Ricky. "We knew that the hiding-place was in this hall, and now we have the clue."

" 'By our Luck.' " Rupert looked about him thoughtfully. "That's not the most helpful—"

"Rupert!" Ricky seized him by the arm. "There's only one thing in this room that will answer that. Can't you see? The niche of the Luck!"

Their gaze followed her pointing finger to the mantel above their heads.

"I believe she's right! Wait until I get the stepladder from the kitchen." Rupert was gone almost before he had finished speaking.

"Oh, if it's only true!" Ricky stared up like one hypnotized. "Then we'll be rich and—"

"Don't count your chickens before they're hatched," Val reminded her, but he didn't think that she heard him.

Then Rupert was back with the ladder. He climbed up, leaving the three of them clustered about its foot.

"Nothing here but two stone studs to hold the Luck in place," he said a moment later.

"Why not try pressing those?" suggested Charity.

"All right, here goes." He placed his thumbs in the corners of the niche and threw his weight upon them.

"Nothing happened." Ricky's voice was deep with disappointment.

"Look!" Val pointed over her shoulder.

To the left of the fireplace were five panels of oak, to balance those on the other side about the door of the unused drawing-room. The center one of these now gaped open, showing a dark cavity.

"It worked!" Ricky was already heading for the opening.

There behind the paneling was a shallow closet which ran the full length of the five panels. It was filled with a collection of bags and small chests, a collection which appeared much larger when it lay in the gloom within than when they dragged it out. Then, when they had time to examine it carefully, they discovered that their booty consisted of two small wooden boxes or chests, one fancifully carved and evidently intended for jewels, the other plain but locked; a felt bag and another of canvas, and a package hurriedly done up in cloth. Rupert spread it all out on the floor.

"Well," he hesitated, "where shall we begin?"

"Charity thought about how to open it, and it was her cat that found us the clue—let her choose," Val suggested.

"Good," agreed Rupert. "And what's your choice, m'lady?"

"What woman could resist this?" She laid her hand upon the jewel box.

"Then that it is." He reached for it.

It opened readily enough to show a shallow tray divided into compartments, all of them empty.

"Sold again," Val commented dryly.

Carefully Rupert lifted out the top tray to disclose another on which rested three small leather bags. He loosened the draw-string of the nearest and shook out into his palm a pair of earrings of a quaint pattern in twisted gold set with dull red stones. Charity pronounced them garnets. Though they were not of great value, they were precious in Ricky's eyes, and even Charity exclaimed over them.

The second bag yielded a carnelian seal on a wide chain of gold mesh, the sort of ornament a dandy wore dangling from his watch pocket in the days of the Regency. And the third bag contained a cross of silver, blackened by time,

97

set with amethysts. This was accompanied by a chain of the same dull metal.

Putting these into the girls' hands, Rupert lifted the second tray to lay bare the bottom of the chest. Here again were several small bags. There was another cross, this time of jet inlaid with gold and attached to a short necklace of jet beads; a wide bracelet of coral and turquoise which was crudely made and might have been native work of some sort. Then there was a tiny jewel-set bottle, about which, Ricky declared, there still lingered some faint trace of the fragrance it had once held. And most interesting to Charity was a fan, the sticks carved of ivory so intricately that they resembled lacework stiffened into slender ribs. The covering between them was fashioned of layers of silk painted with a scene of the bayou country, with the moss-grown oaks and encroaching swamp all carefully depicted.

Charity declared that she had never seen its equal and that some great artist must have decorated the dainty trifle. She closed it carefully and slipped it back into its covering, and Rupert took out the last of the bags. From its depths rolled a ring.

It was plain enough, a simple band of gold so deep in shade as to be almost red. Nearly an inch in width, there was no ornamentation of any sort on its broad, smooth surface.

"Do you know what this is?" Rupert turned the circlet around in his fingers.

"No." Ricky was still dangling the earrings before her eyes.

"It is the wedding-ring of the Bride of the Luck."

"What!" Val leaned forward to look down at the plain circle of gold.

Even Ricky gave her brother her full attention now. Rupert turned to Charity.

"You probably know the story of our Luck?" he asked. She nodded.

"When the Luck was brought from Palestine, it was decided that it must be given into the hands of a guardian who would be responsible for it with his or her life. Because the men of the house were always at war during those troublesome times, the guardianship went to the eldest daughter if she were a maiden. By high and solemn ceremony she was married to the Luck in the chapel of Lorne. And she was the Bride of the Luck until death or a unanimous consent from the family released her. Nor could she marry a mortal husband during the time she wore this." He touched the ring he held.

"This must be very old. It's the red gold which was found in Ireland and England before the Romans conquered the land. Perhaps this was found in some old barrow on Lorne lands. But it no longer means anything without the Luck."

He held it out to Ricky. "By tradition this is yours."

She shook her head. "I don't think I want that, Rupert. It's too old—too strange. Now these," she held up the earrings, "you can understand. The girls who wore them were like me, and they wore them because they were pretty. But that—" she looked at the Bride's ring with distaste—"that must have been a burden to its wearer. Didn't you tell us once of the Lady Iseult, who killed herself when they would not release her from her vows to the Luck? I don't want to wear that, ever.''

"Very well." He dropped it back into its bag. "We'll send it to LeFleur for safe-keeping. Any scruples about the rest of this stuff?''

"Of course not! And none of it is worth much. May I keep it?''

"If you wish. Now let's see what is in here." He drew the second box toward him and forced it open.

"Money!" Charity was staring at it with wide eyes.

Within, in neat bundles, lay packages of paper notes. Even Rupert was shaken from his calm as he reached for one. Outside of a bank none of them had ever seen such a display of wealth. But after he studied the top note, the master of Pirate's Haven laughed thinly.

"This may be worth ten cents to some collector if we're lucky—''

"Rupert! That's real money," began Ricky.

But Val, too, had seen the print. "Confederate money, child. As useless now as our pretty oil stock. I told you that things always turn out wrong in this house. If we do find treasure, it's worthless. How much is there, anyway?''

Rupert picked up a slip of paper tucked under the tape fastening the first bundle. "This says thirty-five thousand— profit from a blockade runner's trip.''

"Thirty-five thousand! Well, I think that that is just too much," Ricky said defiantly. "Why didn't they get paid in real money?''

"Being loyal to the South, the Ralestones probably

would not take what you call 'real money,' " replied Charity.

"It's nice to know how wealthy we once were," Val observed. "What are you going to do with that wall-paper, Rupert?"

"Oh, chuck it in my desk. I'll get someone to look it over; there might be a collector's item among these bills. Now let's have the joker out of *this* bundle." He plucked at the fastenings of the felt bag.

When he had pulled off its wrappings, a silver tray with coffee- and chocolate-pot, cream pitcher and sugar bowl stood, tarnished and dingy, on the floor.

"That's more like it." Ricky picked up the chocolate-pot. "Do you supoose it will ever be possible to get these clean again?"

"With a lot of will power and some good hard rubbing it can be done," Val assured her.

"Well, I'll supply the will power and you may do the rubbing," she announced pleasantly.

Rupert had opened the remaining packages to display a set of twelve silver goblets, one with a dented edge, and a queerly shaped vessel not unlike an old-fashioned gravy-boat. Charity picked this up and examined it gravely.

"I'm afraid that this is pirate loot." She tapped the lip of the piece she held. The metal gave off a clear ringing sound. "If I'm not mistaken, this was stolen from a church. Yes, I'm right; see this cross under the leaves?" She pointed out the bit of engraving.

"Black Dick's work," agreed Ricky complacently. "But after almost three hundred years I'm afraid we can't return it. Especially since we don't know where it came from in the first place.''

Val looked about at what they had uncovered. "If you are going to take all of this in to LeFleur, you'll have to get a truck. D'you know, I think this place might turn out to be a gold-mine if one knew just where to dig.''

"We haven't found the Luck yet," reminded Ricky.

Val got clumsily to his feet and then gave Charity a hand up, beating Rupert to it by about three seconds. "As we don't even know whether it is still in existence, there's no use in hunting for it," Val retorted.

Ricky smiled, that set little smile which usually meant that she neither agreed with nor approved of the speaker. She got up from the floor and shook out her skirt purposefully.

"I'll remind you of that some day," she promised.

"I suppose," Rupert glanced at the silver, "this ought to be taken to town as soon as possible. This house is too isolated to harbor both us and the silverware at the same time. What do you think?" Ignoring both Ricky and Val, he turned to Charity.

"You are right. But it seems a pity to send it all away before we have a chance to rub it up and see what it really looks like!''

"By all means, take it at once!" Val urged promptly. "We can always clean it later.''

Rupert grinned. "Now that might be a protest against the suggestion Ricky made a few minutes ago. But I'll save you some honest labor this time, Val; I'll take it to town this afternoon.''

Ricky laughed softly.

"And why the merriment?" her younger brother inquired suspiciously.

"I was just thinking what a surprise the visitor who dropped his handkerchief here is going to get when he finds the cupboard bare," she explained.

Rupert rubbed his palm across his chin. "Of course. I had almost forgotten that."

"Well, I haven't! And I wonder if we have found what he—or they—were hunting," Val mused as he helped Rupert wrap up the spoil again.

8

GREAT-UNCLE RICK WALKS
THE HALL

Sam had produced a horse complete with saddle and a reputed skittishness. That horse was the pride of Sam's big heart. It had once won a small purse at some country fair or something of the sort, and since then it had been kept only to wear the saddle at rare intervals. Not that Sam ever rode. He drove a spring-board behind a thin, sorrowful mule called "Suggah." But the saddle horse was rented at times to folks of whom Sam approved.

Soon after the arrival of the Ralestones at Pirate's Haven, Sam had brought this four-footed prodigy to their attention. But claiming that the family were his "folks," he indignantly refused to accept hire and was hurt if one of them did not ride at least once a day. Ricky had developed an interest in the garden and had accepted the loan of Sam's eldest son, a boy about as tall as the spade, to help her mess about. Rupert spent the largest part of his days shut up in Bluebeard's chamber. Which of course left the horse to Val.

And Val was becoming slightly bored with Louisiana, at least with that portion of it which immediately surrounded them. Charity was hard at work on her picture of the swamp hunter, for Jeems had come back without warning from his mysterious concerns in the swamp. There was no one to talk to and nowhere to go.

LeFleur had notified them that he believed he was on the track of some discreditable incident in the past of their rival which would banish him from their path. And no more handkerchiefs had been found, ownerless, in their hall. It was a serene morning.

But, Val thought long afterwards, he should have been warned by that very serenity and remembered the old saying, that it was always calmest before a storm. On the contrary, he was riding Sam's horse along the edge of that swamp, wondering what lay hidden back in that dark jungle. Some day, he determined, he would do a little exploring in that direction.

A heron arose from the bayou and streaked across the metallic blue of the sky. Another was wading along, intent upon its fishing. Sam's yellow dog, which had followed horse and rider, set up a barking, annoyed at the haughty carriage of the bird. He scrambled down the steep bank, drove it into flight after its fellow.

Val pulled his shirt away from his sticky skin and wondered if he would ever feel really cool again. There was something about this damp heat which seemed to remove all ambition. He marveled how Ricky could even think of trimming roses that morning.

Sam's dog began to bark deafeningly again, and Val looked around for the heron which must have aroused his displeasure. There was none. But across the swamp crawled an ungainly monster.

Four great rubber-tired wheels, ten feet high, as he later learned, supported a metal framework upon which squatted two men and the driver of the monstrosity. With the ponderous solemnity of a tank it came on to the bayou.

Val's mount snorted and his ears pricked back. He began to have very definite ideas about what he saw. The thing slipped down the marshy bank and took to the water with ease, turning its square nose downstream and sending waves shoreward.

"Ride 'em cowboy!" yelled one of the men derisively as Sam's horse decided to stand on his hind legs and wave at the strange apparition as it went by. Val brought him down upon four feet again, and he stood sweating, his ears still back.

"What do you call that?" the boy shouted back.

"Prospecting engine for swamp use," answered the driver. "Don't you swampers ever get the news?"

The car, or whatever it was, moved on downstream and so out of sight.

"Now I wonder what that means," Val said aloud as his mount sidled toward the center of the road. The hound-dog came up and sat down to kick a patch of flea-invaded territory which lay behind his left ear. Again the morning was quiet.

But not for long. A mud-spattered car came around the bend in the road and headed at Val, going a good pace for the dirt surfacing. Before it quite reached him it stopped and the driver stuck his head out of the window.

"Hey, you, move over! Whatya tryin' to do—break somebody's neck?"

Val surveyed him with interest. The man was, perhaps, Rupert's age, a small, thin fellow with thick black hair and the white seam of an old scar beneath his left eye.

"This is," the boy replied, "a private road."

"Yeah," he snarled, "I know. And I'm the owner. So get your hobby-horse going and beat it, kid."

Val shifted in the saddle and stared down at him.

"And what might your name be?" he asked softly.

"What d'yuh think it is? Hitler? I'm Ralestone, the owner of this place. On your way, kid, on our way."

"So? Well, good morning, cousin." Val tightened rein.

The invader eyed him cautiously. "What d'yuh mean— cousin?"

"I happen to be a Ralestone also," the boy answered grimly.

"Huh? You the guy who thinks he owns this?" he asked aggressively.

"My brother is the present master of Pirate's Haven—"

"That's what *he* thinks," replied the rival with a relish.

"Well, he isn't. That is, not until he pays me for my half. And if he wants to get tough, I'll take it all," he ended, and withdrew into the car like a lizard into its rock den.

Val sat by the side of the road and watched the car slide along toward the plantation. As it passed him he caught a glimpse of a second passenger in the back seat. It was the red-faced man he had seen with LeFleur's clerk on the street in New Orleans. Resolutely Val turned back and started for the house in the wake of the rival.

By making use of a short-cut, he reached the front of the house almost as soon as the car. Ricky had been working with the morning-glory vines about the terrace steps, young Sam standing attendance with a rusty trowel and one of the kitchen forks.

At the sound of the car she stood up and tried to brush a smear of sticky earth from the front of her checked-gingham dress. When the rival got out she smiled at him.

"Hello, sister," he smirked.

She stood still for a moment and her smile faded. When she answered, her voice was chill. "You wished to see Mr. Ralestone?" she asked distantly.

"Sure. But not just yet, sister. You better be pleasant, you know. I'm the new owner here—"

Val rode out of the bushes and swung out of the saddle, coming up behind him. Although the boy was one of the smaller "Black" Ralestones, he topped the invader by a good two inches, and he noted this with delight as he came up to him.

"Ricky," he said briefly, "go in. And send Sam for Rupert."

She nodded and was gone. The man turned to face Val. "You again, huh?" he demanded.

"Yes. And Ralestone or no Ralestone, I would advise you to keep a civil tongue in your head," he began hotly, when Rupert appeared at the door.

"Well, Val," he asked, a frown creasing his forehead, "what is it?"

The rival advanced a short step and looked up. "So you're the guy who's trying to do me out of my rights?"

Rupert reached behind him and closed the screen before coming to the head of the terrace steps. "I presume that you are Mr. Ralestone?" he asked quietly.

" 'Course I'm Ralestone," asserted the other. "And I'm part owner of this place."

"That has not yet been decided," answered Rupert calmly. "But suppose you tell me to what we owe the honor of this visit?"

Now, however, the passenger took a hand in the game. He crawled out of the car, taking off his soiled panama to wipe his bald head with a gaudy silk handkerchief.

"Here, here, Mr. Ralestone," he addressed his companion, "let us have no unpleasantness. We have merely come here today, sir," he explained to Rupert, "to see if matters could not be settled amicably without having to take recourse to a court of law. Your Mr. LeFleur will give us very little satisfaction, you see. I am a plain and honest man, sir, and I believe an affair of this kind may be best agreed upon between principals. My client, Mr. Ralestone, is a reasonable man; he will be moderate in his demands. It will be to your advantage to listen to our proposal. After all, you cannot contest his rights—''

''But that is just what I am going to do.'' Rupert smiled down at them, if a slight twist of the lips may be called a smile. ''Have you ever heard that old saying that 'possession is nine points of the law'? I am the Ralestone in residence, and I shall continue to be the Ralestone in residence until after this case is heard. Now, as I am a busy man and this is the middle of the morning, I shall have to say good-bye—''

''So that's the way you're going to take it?'' The visiting Ralestone glared at Rupert. ''All right. Play it that way and you won't be here a month from now. Nor,'' he turned on Val, ''this kid brother of yours, either. You can't pull this lord-of-the-land stuff on me and get away with it. I'll—'' But he did not finish his threat. Instead, his jaws clamped shut on mid-word. In silence he turned and got into the car to which his counselor had already withdrawn.

The car leaped forward into a rose bush. With a savage twist of the wheel the driver brought it back to the drive, leaving deep prints in the front lawn. Then it was gone, down the drive, as they stood staring after it.

''So that's that,'' Val commented. ''Well, all I've got to say is that Rick's branch of the family has sadly gone to seed—''

''Being a southern gentleman has made you slightly snobbish.'' Ricky came out from her lurking place behind the door.

''Snobbish!'' her brother choked at the injustice. ''I

suppose that that is your idea of a perfect gentleman, a diamond in the rough—''

He pointed down the drive.

Ricky laughed. "It's so easy to tease you, Val. Of course he is a—a wart of the first class. But Rupert will fix him—won't you?''

Her older brother grinned. "After that example of your trust in me, I'll have to. I agree, he is not the sort you would care to introduce to your more particular friends. But this visit seems to suggest something—''

"That he has the wind up?'' Val asked.

"There are indications of that, I think. Something LeFleur has done has stirred our friends into direct action. We shall probably have more of it within the immediate future. So I want you, Ricky, to go to town. Madame LeFleur has very kindly offered to put you up—''

Each tiny curl on Ricky's head seemed to bristle with indignation. "Oh, no you don't, Rupert Ralestone! You don't get me away from here when there are exciting things going on. I hardly think that our friend with the slimy manner will use machine-guns to blast us out. And if he does—well, it wouldn't be the first time that this house was used as a fortress. I'm not going one step out of here unless you two come with me.''

Rupert shrugged. "As I can't very well hog-tie you to get you to town, I suppose you will have to stay. But I *am* going to send for Lucy.'' With that parting shot he turned and went in.

Lucy arrived shortly before noon. She was accompanied

by a portion of her large family—four, Val counted, including that Sam who had become Ricky's faithful shadow.

"What's all this 'bout some man sayin' he is Ralestone?" she demanded of Ricky. "Some policeman oughta lock him up. Effen he comes botherin' 'roun' agin, let me tend to him!"

With that she marched majestically into the kitchen, elbowed Letty-Lou out of her way, and proceeded to stir up a batch of brown molasses cookies. " 'Cause dey is fillin' fo' boys. An' Mistuh Val, heah, he needs some fat 'crost his skinny ribs. Letty-Lou, yo' ain't feedin' dese menfolks ri'. Now yo' chillens," she swooped down upon her own family, "yo'all gits outa heah, don't fuss me."

"They can come with me," offered Ricky. "I'm trying to find that maze which is marked on the garden plans."

"Miss 'Chanda, yo' ain't a'goin' 'way 'afore youah brothah gits through workin'. He done tol' me to keep an eye on yo'all. Why don't yo' go visit wi' Miss Charity?"

Ricky looked at her watch. "All right. She'll be through her morning work by now. I'll take the children, Lucy."

To Val's open surprise, she obeyed Lucy, meekly moving off without a single protest. One of the boys remained behind and offered shyly to take the horse back to Sam's place. When Lucy agreed that it would be all right, Val boosted him into the saddle where he clung like a jockey.

"An' wheah is yo' goin', Mistuh Val?" asked Lucy, cutting out round cookies with a downward stroke of the drinking glass she had pressed into service. The regular cutter was, in her opinion, too small.

"Down toward the bayou. I'll be back before lunch,"

he said, and hurried out before she could as definitely dispose of him as she had of Ricky.

Val struck off into the bushes until he came to one of the paths that crossed the wilderness. As it ran in the direction of the bayou, he turned into it. Then for the second time he came into the glen of the pool and passed along the path Jeems had known. So somehow Val was not surprised, when he came out upon the edge of the bayou levee, to see Jeems sitting there.

"Hello!" The swamper looked up at Val's hail but this time he did not leave.

"Hullo," he answered sullenly.

Val stood there, ill at ease, while the swamper eyed him composedly. What could he say now? Val's embarrassment must have been very apparent, for after a long moment Jeems smiled derisively.

"Yo' goin' ridin' in them funny pants?" he asked, pointing to the other's breeches.

"Well, that's what they are intended for," Val replied.

"Wheah's youah hoss?"

"I sent him back to Sam's." Val was beginning to feel slightly warm. He decided that Jeems' manners were not all that they might be.

"Sam!" the swamp boy spat into the water. "He's a—"

But what Sam was, in the opinion of the swamper, Val never learned, for at that moment Ricky burst from between two bushes.

"Well, at last," she panted, "I've gotten rid of my

army. Val, do you think that Lucy is going to be like this all the time—order us about, I mean?''

"Who's that?" Jeems was on his feet looking at Ricky.

"Ricky," her brother said, "this is Jeems. My sister Richanda."

"Yo' one of the folks up at the big house?" he asked her directly.

"Why, yes," she answered simply.

"Yo' don' act like yo' was." He stabbed his finger at both of them. "Yo' don't walk with youah noses in the air looking down at us—"

"Of course we don't!" interrupted Ricky. "Why should we, when you know more about this place than we do?"

"What do yo' mean by that?" he flashed out at her, his sullen face suddenly dark.

"Why— why—" Ricky faltered, "Charity Biglow said that you knew all about the swamp—"

His tense position relaxed a fraction. "Oh, yo' know Miss Charity?"

"Yes. She showed us the picture she is painting, the one you are posing for," Ricky went on.

"Miss Charity is a fine lady," he returned with conviction. He shifted from one bare foot to the other. "Ah'll be goin' now." With no other farewell he slipped over the side of the levee into his canoe and headed out into midstream. Nor did he look back.

Lucy departed after dinner that evening to bed down her family before returning with Letty-Lou to occupy one of the servant's rooms over the side wing. Rupert had gone with her to interview Sam. Val gathered that Sam had some notion of trying to reintroduce the growing of indigo, a crop which had been forsaken for sugar-cane at the beginning of the nineteenth century when a pest had destroyed the entire indigo crop of that year all over Louisiana.

"Let's go out in the garden," suggested Ricky.

"What for?" asked her brother. "To provide a free banquet for mosquitoes? No, thank you, let's stay here."

"You're lazy," she countered.

"You may call it laziness; I call it prudence," he answered.

"Well, I'm going anyway," she made a decision which brought Val reluctantly to his feet. For mosquitoes or no mosquitoes, he was not going to allow Ricky to be outside alone.

They followed the path which led around the side of the house until it neared the kitchen door. When they reached that point Ricky halted.

"Listen!"

A plaintive miaow sounded from the kitchen.

"Oh, bother! Satan's been left inside. Go and let him out."

"Will you stay right here?" Val asked.

"Of course. Though I don't see why you and Rupert have taken to acting as if Fu Manchu were loose in our yard. Now hurry up before he claws the screen to pieces. Satan, I mean, not the sinister Chinese gentleman."

But Satan did not meet Val at the door. Apparently, having received no immediate answer to his plea, he had withdrawn into the bulk of the house. Speaking unkind things about him under his breath, Val started across the dark kitchen.

Suddenly he stopped. He felt the solid edge of the table against his thigh. When he put out his hand he touched the reassuring everyday form of Lucy's stone cooky jar. He was in their own pleasant everyday kitchen.

But—

He was not alone in that house!

There had been the faintest of sounds from the forepart of the main section, a sound such as Satan might have caused. But Val knew—knew positively—that Satan was guiltless. Someone or something was in the Long Hall.

He crept by the table, hoping that he could find his way without running into anything. His hand closed upon the knob of the door opening upon the back stairs used by Letty-Lou. If he could get up them and across the upper hall, he could come down the front stairs and catch the intruder.

It took Val perhaps two minutes to reach the head of the front stairs, and each minute seemed a half-hour in length. From below he could hear a regular *pad, pad*, as if from stocking feet on the stone floor. He drew a deep breath and started down.

When he reached the landing he looked over the rail. Upright before the fire-place was a dim white blur. As he watched, it moved forward. There was something uncanny about that almost noiseless movement.

The blur became a thin figure clad in baggy white breeches and loose shirt. Below the knees the legs seemed to fade into the darkness of the hall and there was something strange about the outlines of the head.

Again the thing resumed its padding and Val saw now that it was pacing the hall in a regular pattern. Which suggested that it was human and was there with a very definite purpose.

He edged farther down the stairs.

"And just what are you doing?"

If his voice quavered upon the last word, it was hardly his fault. For when the thing turned, Val saw—

It had no face!

With a startled cry he lunged forward, clutching at the banister to steady his blundering descent. The thing backed away; already it was fading into the darkness beside the stairs. As Val's feet touched the floor of the hall he caught his last glimpse of it, a thin white patch against the solid paneling of the stairway's broad side. Then it was gone. When Rupert and Ricky came in a few minutes later and turned on the lights, Val was still staring at that blank wall, with Satan rubbing against his ankles.

9

PORTRAIT OF A LADY AND A
GENTLEMAN

Rupert had dismissed Val's story of what he had seen in
the hall in a very lofty manner. When his brother had
persisted in it, Rupert suggested that Val had better keep
out of the sun in the morning. For no trace of the thing
which had troubled the house remained.

Ricky hesitated between believing wholly in Val's tale
or just in his powers of imagination. And between them
his family drove him sulky to bed. He was still frowning,
or maybe it was a new frown, when he looked into the
bathroom mirror the next morning as he dressed. For Val
knew that he *had* seen something in the hall, something
monstrous which had no right to be there.

What had their rival said before he left? "Play it that way and you won't be here a month from now." It was just possible— Val paused, half in, half out of, his shirt. Could last night's adventure have had anything to do with that threat? Two or three episodes of that sort might unsettle the strongest nerves and drive the occupants from a house where such a shadow walked.

Something else nagged at the boy's memory. Slowly he traced back over the events of the day before, from the moment when he had watched that queer swamp car crawl downstream. After the visit of the rival, Lucy had come to stay. And then Ricky had started for Charity's while he had gone down to the bayou where he met Jeems. That was it. Jeems!

When Ricky had hinted that he knew more of the swamp than the Ralestones did, why had he been so quick to resent that remark? Could it be because he understood her to mean that he knew more of Pirate's Haven than they did?

And the thing in the Long Hall last night had known of some exit in the wall that the Ralestones did not know of. It had faded into the base of the staircase. And yet, when Val had gone over the paneling there inch by inch, he had gained nothing but sore finger tips.

He tucked his shirt under his belt and looked down to see if Sam Junior had polished his boots as Lucy had ordered her son to do. Save for a trace of mud by the right heel, they had the proper mirror-like surface.

"Mistuh Val," Lucy's penetrating voice made him start guiltily, "is yo' or is yo' not comin' to breakfas'?"

"I am," he answered and started downstairs at his swiftest pace.

The new ruler of their household was standing at the foot of the stairs, her knuckles resting on her broad hips. She eyed the boy sternly. Lucy eyed one, Val thought, much as a Scotch nurse Ricky and he had once had. They had never dared question any of Annie's decrees, and one look from her had been enough to reduce them to instant order. Lucy's eye had the same power. And now as she herded Val into the dining-room he felt like a six-year-old with an uneasy conscience.

Rupert and Ricky were already seated and eating. That is, Ricky was eating, but Rupert was reading his morning mail.

"Yo'all sits down," said Lucy firmly, "an' yo'all eats what's on the plate. Yo' ain' much fattah then a jay-bird."

"I don't see why she keeps comparing me to a living skeleton all the time," Val complained as she departed kitchenward.

"She told Letty-Lou yesterday," supplied Ricky through a mouthful of popover, "that you are 'peaked lookin'.' "

"Why doesn't she start in on Rupert? He needs another ten pounds or so." Val reached for the butter. "And he hasn't got a very good color, either." Val surveyed his brother professionally. "Doesn't get outdoors enough."

"No," Ricky's voice sounded aggrieved, "he's too busy having secrets—"

"Hmm," Rupert murmured, more interested in his letter than in the conversation.

"The trouble is that we are not Chinese bandits, Malay pirates, or Arab freebooters. We don't possess color, life, enough—enough—"

"Sugar," Rupert interrupted Val, pushing his coffee-cup in the general direction of Ricky without raising his eyes from the page in his hand. She giggled.

"So that's what we lack. Well, now we know. How much sugar should we have, Rupert? Rupert—Mr. Rupert Ralestone—Mr. Rupert Ralestone of Pirate's Haven!" Her voice grew louder and shriller until he did lay down his reading matter and really looked at them for the first time.

"What do you want?"

"A little attention," answered Ricky sweetly. "We aren't Chinese, Arabs, or Malays, but we are kind of nice to know, aren't we, Val? If you'd only come out of your subconscious, or wherever you are most of the time, you'd find that out without being told."

Rupert laughed and pushed away his letters. "Sorry. I picked up the bad habit of reading at breakfast when I didn't have my table brightened by your presence. I know," he became serious, "that I haven't been much of a family man. But there are reasons—"

"Which, of course, you can not tell *us*," flashed Ricky.

His face lengthened ruefully. He pulled at his tie with an embarrassed frown. "Not yet, anyway. I—" He fumbled with his napkin. "Oh, well, let me see how it comes out first."

Ricky opened her eyes to their widest extent and leaned forward, every inch of her expressing awe. "Rupert, don't tell me that you are an *inventor!*" she cried.

"Now I know that we'll end in the poorhouse," Val observed.

Rupert had recovered his composure. " 'I yam what I yam,' " he quoted.

"Very well. Keep it to yourself then," pouted Ricky. "We can have secrets too."

"I don't doubt it." He glanced at Val. "Unfortunately you always tell them. See any more bogies last night, Val? Did a big, black, formless something reach out from under the bed and clutch at you?"

But his brother refused to be drawn. "No, but when it does I'll sic it onto you. A big, black, formless something is just what you need. And I'll—"

"Am I interrupting?" Charity stood in the door.

"Goodness! Haven't you finished breakfast yet? Do you people know that it is almost ten?"

"Madam, we have banished time." Rupert drew out the chair at his left. "Will you favor us with your company?"

"I thought you were going to be busy today," said Ricky as she rang for Letty-Lou and a fresh cup of coffee for their guest.

"So did I," sighed Charity. "And I should be. I've got this order, you know, and now I can't get any models. Why there should be a sudden dearth of them right now, I can't imagine. I thought I could use Jeems again, but somehow he isn't the type." She raised her cup to her lips.

"Are you doing story illustrations?" asked Rupert, more alive now than he had been all morning.

"Yes. A historical thriller for a magazine. They want a

full-page cut for the first chapter and a half-page to illustrate the most exciting scene. Then there're innumerable smaller ones. But the two large ones are what I'm worrying about. I like to get the important stuff finished first, and now I simply can't get models who are the right types."

"What's the story about?" demanded Ricky.

"It's laid in Haiti during the French invasion led by Napoleon's brother-in-law, the one who married Pauline. All voodoo and aristocratic young hero and beautiful maiden pursued by an officer of the black rebels. And," she almost wailed, "here I am with the clothes apread all over my bed—the right costumes, you know—with no one to wear them. I went over to the Corners this morning and called Johnson—he runs a registration office for models—but he couldn't promise me anyone." She bit absent-mindedly into a round spiced roll Ricky had placed before her.

"Wait!" She laid down the roll in a preoccupied fashion and stared across the table. "Val, stand up."

Wondering, he pushed back his chair and arose obediently.

"Turn your head a little more to the right," Charity ordered. "There, that's it! Now try to look as if there were something all ready to spring at you from that corner over there."

For one angry moment he thought that she had been told of what had happened the night before and was baiting him, as the others had done. But a sidewise glance showed him that her interest lay elsewhere. So he screwed up his features into what he fondly hoped was a grim and deadly smile.

"For goodness sake, don't look as if you had eaten green apples," Ricky shot at him. "Just put on that face you wear when I show you a new hat. No, not that sneering one; the other."

Rupert threw back his head and laughed heartily. "Better let him alone, Ricky. After all, it's *his* face."

"I'm glad that someone has pointed out that fact," Val said stiffly, "because—"

"Oh, be quiet!" Charity leaned forward across the table. "Yes," she nodded, "you'll do."

"For what?" Val asked, slightly apprehensive.

"For my hero. Of course your hair is too short and you are rather too youthful, but I can disguise those points. And," she turned upon Ricky, "you can be the lady in distress. Which gives me another idea. Do you suppose that I might use your terrace for a background and have that big chair, the one with the high back?" she asked Rupert.

"You may have anything you want within these walls," he answered lightly enough, but it was clear that he really meant it.

"What am I supposed to do?" Val asked.

Charity considered. "I think I'll try the action one first," she said half to herself. "That's going to be the most difficult. Ricky, will you send one of Lucy's children over with me to help carry back the costumes and my material—" She was already at the door.

"Val and I will go instead," Ricky replied.

Some twenty minutes later Val was handed a suitcase and told to use the contents to cover his back. Having doubts of the wisdom of the whole affair, he went reluctantly upstairs to obey. But the result was not so bad. The broad-shouldered, narrow-waisted coat did not fit him ill, though the shiny boots were at least a size too large. Timidly he went down. Ricky was the first to see him.

"Val! You look like something out of a Regency novel. Rupert, look at Val. Doesn't he look wonderful?"

Having thus made public his embarrassment, she ran to the mirror to finish her own prinking. The high-waisted Empire gown of soft green voile made her appear taller than usual. But she walked with a little shuffle which suggested that her ribbon-strapped slippers fitted her no better than Val's boots did him. Charity was coaxing Ricky's tight fashionable curls into a looser arrangement and tying a green ribbon about them. This done, she turned to survey Val.

"I thought so," she said with satisfaction. "You are just what I want. But," the tiny lines about her eyes crinkled in amusement, "at present you are just a little too perfect. Do you realize that you have just fought off an attack, led by a witch doctor, in which you were wounded; that you have struggled through a jungle for seven hours in order to reach your betrothed; and that you are now facing death by torture? I hardly think that you should look as if you had just stepped out of the tailor's—"

"I've done all that?" Val demanded, somewhat staggered.

125

"Well, the author says you have, so you've got to look it. We'd better muss you up a bit. Let's see." She tapped her fingernails against her teeth as she looked him up and down. "Off with that coat first."

He wriggled out of the coat and stood with the glories of his ruffled shirt fully displayed. "Now what?" he asked.

"This," she reached forward and ripped his left sleeve to the shoulder. "Untie that cravat and take it off. Roll up your other sleeve above the elbow. That's right. Ricky, you muss up his hair. Let a lock of it fall across his forehead. No, not there—there. Good. Now he's ready for the final touches." She went to the table where her paints had been left. "Let's see—carmine, that ought to be right. This is water-color, Val, it'll all wash off in a minute."

Across his smooth tanned cheek she dribbled a jagged line of scarlet. Then instructing Ricky to bind the torn edge of his sleeve above his elbow, she also stained the bandage. "Well?" she turned to Rupert.

"He looks as though he had been through the wars all right," he agreed. "But what about the costume?"

"Oh, we needn't worry about that. They knew I'd have to do this, so they duplicated everything. Now for you, Ricky. Pull your sleeve down off your shoulder and see if you can tear the skirt up from the hem on that side—about as far as your knee. Yes, that's fine. You're ready now."

Rupert picked up from the table a sword and a long-barrelled dueling pistol and led the way out onto the terrace. Charity pointed to the big chair in the sunlight.

"This will probably be hard for you two," she warned

them frankly. "If you get tired, don't hesitate to tell me. I'll give you a rest every ten minutes. Val, you sit down in the chair. Slump over toward that arm as if you were about finished. No, more limp than that. Now look straight ahead. You are on the terrace of Beauvallet. Beside you is the girl you love. You are all that stands between her and the black rebels. Now take this sword in your right hand and the pistol in your left. Lean forward a little. There! Now don't move; you've got just the pose I want. Ricky, crouch down by the side of his chair with your arm up so that you can touch his hand. You're terrified. There's death, horrible death, before you!"

Val could feel Ricky's hand quiver against his. Charity had made them both see and feel what she wanted them to. They weren't in the peaceful sunlight on the terrace of Pirate's Haven; they were miles farther south in the dark land of Haiti, the Haiti of more than a hundred years ago. Before them was a semitropical forest from which at any moment might crawl—death. Val's hand tightened on the sword hilt; the pistol butt was clammy in his grip.

Rupert had put up the easel and laid out the paints. And now, taking up her charcoal, Charity began to sketch with clear, clean strokes.

Her models' unaccustomed muscles cramped so that when they shifted during their rest periods they grimaced with pain. Ricky whispered that she did not wonder models were hard to get. After a while Rupert went away without Charity noticing his leaving. The sun burned Val's cheek where the paint had dried and he felt a trickle of moisture edge down his spine. But Charity worked on, thoroughly intent upon what was growing under her brushes.

It must have been close to noon when she was at last interrupted.

"Hello there, Miss Biglow!"

Two men stood below the terrace on a garden path. One of them waved his hat as Charity looked around. And behind them stood Jeems.

"Go away," said the worker, "go away, Judson Holmes. I haven't any time for you today."

"Not after I've come all the way from New York to see you?" he asked reproachfully. "Why, Charity!" He had the reddest hair Val had ever seen—and the homeliest face—but his small-boy grin was friendliness itself.

"Go away," she repeated stubbornly.

"Nope!" He shook his head firmly. "I'm staying right here until you forget that for at least a minute." He motioned toward the picture.

With a sigh she put down her brush. "I suppose I'll have to humor you."

"Miss Charity," Jeems had not taken his eyes from the two models since he had arrived and he did not move them now, "what're they all fixed up like that fur?"

"It's a picture for a story," she explained. "A story about Haiti in the old days—"

"Ah reckon Ah know," he nodded eagerly, his face suddenly alight. "That's wheah th' blacks kilt th' French back in history times. Ah got me a book 'bout it. A book in handwritin', not printin,. Père Armand larned me to read it."

128

Judson Holmes' companion moved forward. "A book in handwriting," he said slowly. "Could that possibly mean a diary?"

Charity was wiping her hands on a paint rag. "It might. New Orleans was a port of refuge for a great many of the French who fled the island during the slave uprising. It is not impossible."

"I've got to see it! Here, boy, what's your name?" He pounced upon Jeems. "Can you get that book here this afternoon?"

Jeems drew back. "Ah ain't gonna bring no book heah. That's mine an' you ain't gonna set eye on it!" With that parting shot he was gone.

"But—but—" protested the other, "I've got to see it. Why, such a find might be priceless."

Mr. Holmes laughed. "Curb your hunting instincts for once, Creighton. You can't handle a swamper that way. Let's go and see Charity's masterpiece instead."

"I don't remember having asked you to," she observed.

"Oh, see here now, wasn't I the one who got you this commission? And Creighton here is that strange animal known as a publisher's scout. And publishers sometimes desire the services of illustrators, so you had better impress Creighton as soon as possible. Well," he looked at the picture, "you have done it!"

Even Creighton, who had been inclined to stare back over his shoulder at the point where Jeems disappeared, now gave it more than half his attention.

"Is that for *Drums of Doom?*" he asked becoming suddenly crisp and professional.

129

"Yes."

"Might do for the jacket of the book. Have Mr. Richards see this. Marvelous types, where did you get them?" he continued, looking from the canvas to Ricky and Val.

"Oh, I am sorry. Miss Ralestone, may I present Mr. Creighton, and Mr. Holmes, both of New York. And this," she smiled at Val, "is Mr. Valerius Ralestone, the brother of the owner of this plantation. The family, I believe, has lived here for about two hundred and fifty years."

Creighton's manner became a shade less brusque as he took the hand Ricky held out to him. "I might have known that no professional could get that look," he said.

"Then this isn't your place?" Mr. Holmes said to Charity after he had greeted the Ralestones.

"Mine? Goodness no! I rent the old overseer's house. Pirate's Haven is Ralestone property."

"Pirate's Haven." Judson Holmes' infectious grin reappeared. "A rather suggestive name."

"The builder intended to name it 'King's Acres' because it was a royal grant," Val informed him. "But he was a pirate, so the other name was given it by the country folk and he adopted it. And he was right in doing so because there were other freebooters in the family after his time."

"Yes, we are even equipped with a pirate ghost," contributed Ricky with a mischievous glance in her brother's direction.

Holmes fanned himself with his hat. "So romance isn't

dead after all. Well, Charity, shall we stay—in town I mean?"

"Why?" a thin line appeared between her eyes as if she had little liking for such a plan.

"Well, Creighton is here on the track of a mysterious new writer who is threatening to produce a second *Gone with the Wind*. And I—well, I like the climate."

"We'll see," muttered Charity.

10

INTO THE SWAMP

In spite of the fact that they received but lukewarm encouragement from Charity, both Holmes and Creighton lingered on in New Orleans. Mr. Creighton made several attempts to get in touch with Jeems, whom he seemed to suspect of concealing vast literary treasures. And he spent one hot morning going through the trunk of papers which the Ralestones had found in the storage-room. Ricky commented upon the fact that being a publisher's scout was almost like being an antique buyer.

Holmes was a perfect foil for his laboring friend. He lounged away his days draped across the settee on Charity's gallery or sitting down on the bayou levee—after she had chased him away—pitching pebbles into the water. He told all of them that it was his vacation, the first one he had had in five years, and that he was going to make the most of it. Companioned by Creighton, he usually enlarged the family circle in the evenings. And the tales he could tell about the far corners of the earth were as wildly romantic as Rupert's—though he did assure his listeners that even Tibet was very tame and well behaved nowadays.

Charity had finished the first illustration and had started another. This time Ricky and Val appeared polished and combed as if they had just stepped out of a ball-room of a governor's palace—which they had, according to the story. It was during her second morning's work upon this that she threw down her brush with a snort of disgust.

"It's no use," she told her models, "I simply can't work on this now. All I can see is that scene where the hero's mulatto half-brother watches the ball from the underbrush. I've got to do that one first."

"Why don't you then?" Ricky stretched to relieve cramped muscles.

"I would if I could get Jeems. He's my model for the brother. He's enough like you, Val, for the resemblance, and his darker tan is just right for color. But he won't come back while Creighton's here. I could wring that man's neck!"

"But Creighton left for Milneburg this morning," Val reminded her. "Rupert told him about the old voodoo rites which used to be celebrated there on June 24th, St. John's Eve, and he wanted to see if there were any records—"

"Yes. But Jeems doesn't know he's gone. If we could only get in touch with him—Jeems, I mean."

"Miss 'Chanda!"

Sam Two, as they had come to call Sam's eldest son and heir, was standing on the lowest step of the terrace, holding a small covered basket in his hands.

"Yes?"

"Letty-Lou say this am fo' yo', Miss 'Chanda."

"For me?" Ricky looked at the offering in surprise. "But what in the world—Bring it here, Sam."

"Yas'm."

He laid the basket in Ricky's outstretched hands.

"I've never seen anything like this before." She turned it around. "It seems to be woven of some awfully fine grass—"

"That's swamp work." Charity was peering over Ricky's shoulder. "Open it."

Inside on a nest of raw wild cotton lay a bracelet of polished wood carved with an odd design of curling lines which reminded Val of Spanish moss. And with the circlet was a small purse of scaled hide.

"Swamp oak and baby alligator," burst out Charity. "Aren't they beauties?"

"But who—" began Ricky.

Val picked up a scrap of paper which had fluttered to the floor. It was cheap stuff, ruled with faint blue lines, but the writing was bold and clear: "Miss Richanda Ralestone."

"It's yours all right." He handed her the paper.

134

"I know." She tucked the note away with the gifts. "It was Jeems."

"Jeems? But why?" her brother protested.

"Well, yesterday when I was down by the levee he was coming in and I knew that Mr. Creighton was here and I told him. So," she colored faintly, "then he took me across the bayou and I got some of those big swamp lilies that I've always wanted. And we had a long talk. Val, Jeems knows the most wonderful things about the swamps. Do you know that they still have voodoo meetings sometimes—way back in there," she swept her hand southward. "And the fur trappers live on houseboats, renting their hunting rights. But Jeems owns his own land. Now some northerners are prospecting for oil. They have a queer sort of car which can travel either on land or water. And Père Armand has church records that date back to the middle of the eighteenth century. And—"

"So that's where you were from four until almost six," Val laughed. "I don't know that I approve of this riotous living. Will Jeems take me to pick the lilies too?"

"Maybe. He wanted to know why you always moved so carefully. And I told him about the accident. Then he said the oddest thing—" She was staring past Val at the oaks. "He said that to fly was worth being smashed up for and that he envied you."

"Then he's a fool!" her brother said promptly. "Nothing is worth—" Val stopped abruptly. Five months before he had made a bargain with himself; he was not going to break it now.

"Do you know," Ricky said to Charity, "if you really

135

need Jeems this morning, I think I can get him for you. He told me yesterday how to find his cabin.

"But why—" The objection came almost at once from Charity. Val thought she was more than a little surprised that Jeems, who had steadfastly refused to give her the same information, had supplied it so readily to Ricky whom he hardly knew at all.

"I don't know," answered Ricky frankly. "He was rather queer about it. Kept saying that the time might come when I would need help, and things like that."

"Charity," Val was putting her brushes straight, "I learned long ago that nothing can be kept from Ricky. Sooner or later one spills out his secrets."

"Except Rupert!" Ricky aired her old grievance.

"Perhaps Rupert," her brother agreed.

"Anyway, I do know where Jeems lives. Do you want me to get him for you, Charity?"

"Certainly not, child! Do you think that I'd let you go into the swamp? Why, even men who know something of woodcraft think twice before attempting such a trip without a guide. Of course you're not going! I think," she put her paint-stained hand to her head, "that I'm going to have one of my sick headaches. I'll have to go home and lie down for an hour or two."

"I'm sorry." Ricky's sympathy was quick and warm. "Is there anything I can do?"

Charity shook her head with a rueful smile. "Time is the only medicine for one of these. I'll see you later."

"Just the same," Ricky stood looking after her, "I'd

136

like to know just what is going on in the swamp right now.''

"Why?" Val asked lightly.

"Because—well, just because," was her provoking answer. "Jeems was so odd yesterday. He talked as if—as if there were some threat to us or him. I wonder if there is something wrong." She frowned.

"Of course not!" her brother made prompt answer. "He's merely gone off on one of those mysterious trips of his."

"Just the same, what if there were something wrong? We might go and see."

"Nonsense!" Val snapped. "You heard what Charity said about going into the swamp alone. And there is nothing to worry about anyway. Come on, let's change. And then I have something to show you."

"What?" she demanded.

"Wait and see." His ruse had succeeded. She was no longer looking swampward with that gleam of purpose in her eye.

"Come on then," she said, prodding him into action.

Val changed slowly. If one didn't care about mucking around in the garden, as Ricky seemed to delight in doing, there was so little in the way of occupation. He thought of the days as they spread before him. A little riding, a great amount of casual reading and—what else? Was the South "getting" him as the tropics are supposed to "get" the Northerners?

That unlucky meeting with a mountaintop had effectively despoiled him of his one ambition. Soldiers with

137

game legs are not wanted. He couldn't paint like Charity, he couldn't spin yarns like Rupert, he possessed a mind too inaccurate to cope with the intricacies of any science. And as a business man he would probably be a good street cleaner.

What was left? Well, the surprise he had promised Ricky might cover the problem. As he reached for a certain black note-book, someone knocked on his door.

"Mistuh Val, wheah's Miss 'Chanda? She ain't here, an' Ah wants to—"

Lucy stood in the hall. The light from the round window was reflected from every corrugated wave of her painfully marcelled hair. Her vast flowered dress had been thriftily covered with a dull-green bib-apron and she had changed her smart slippers for the shapeless gray relics she wore indoors. Just now she looked warm and tired. After all, running two households was something of a task even for Lucy.

"Why, she should be in her room. We came up to change. Miss Charity's gone home with a headache. What was it you wanted her for?"

"Mistuh Val"—she thrust a mound of snowy and beruffled white stuff at him—"These curtains has got to be hung. An' does Miss 'Chanda want 'em in her room or not?"

"Better put them up. I'll tell her about it. Here wait, let me open that door."

Val looked into Ricky's room. As usual, it appeared as though a whirlwind, a small whirlwind but a thorough one, had passed through it. Her discarded costume lay tumbled across the bed and her slippers lay on the floor, one upside down. He stooped to set them straight.

"It do beat all," Lucky said frankly as she put her burden down on a chair, "how dat chile make a mess. Now yo', Mistuh Val, jest put everythin' jest so. But Miss 'Chanda leave hers which way afore Sunday! Looka dat now." She pointed to the half-opened door of the closet. A slip lay on the floor. Ricky must have been in a hurry; that was a little too untidy even for her.

A sudden suspicion sent Val into the closet to investigate. Ricky's wardrobe was not so extensive that he did not know every dress and article in it very well. It did not take him more than a moment to see what was missing.

"Did Ricky go riding?" Val asked. "Her habit is gone."

"She ain' gone 'cross de bayo' fo' de hoss," answered Lucky, reaching for the curtain rod. "Anyway, Sam took dat critter to be shoed."

"Then where—" But Val knew his Ricky only too well.

She had a certain stubborn will of her own. Sometimes opposition merely drove her into doing the forbidden thing. And the swamp had been forbidden. But could even Ricky be such a fool? Certain memories of the past testified that she could. But how? Unless she had taken Sam's boat—

Without a word of explanation to Lucy, he dashed out of the room and downstairs at his best pace. As he left the house Val broke into a stumbling run. There was just a chance that she had not yet left the plantation.

But the bayou levee was deserted. And the post where Sam's boat was usually moored was bare of rope; the boat was gone. Of course Sam Two might have taken it across the stream to the farm.

That hope was extinguished as the small brown boy came out of the bushes along the stream side.

"Sam, have you seen Miss 'Chanda?" Val demanded.

"Yessuh."

"Where?" Carrying on a conversation with Sam Two was like prying diamonds out of a rock. He possessed a rooted distaste for talking.

"Heah, suh."

"When?"

"Jest a li'l while ago."

"Where did she go?"

Sam pointed downstream.

"Did she take the boat?"

"Yessuh." And then for the first time since Val had known him Sam volunteered a piece of information. "She say she a-goin' in de swamp."

Val leaned back against the bole of one of the willows. Then she had done it! And what could he do? If he had any idea of her path, he could follow her while Sam aroused Rupert and the house.

"If I only knew where—" he mused aloud.

"She a-goin' to see dat swamper Jeems," Sam continued. "Heh, heh," a sudden cackle of laughter rippled across his lips. "Dat ole swamper think he so sma't. Think no one find his house—"

"Sam!" Val rounded upon him. "Do you know where Jeems lives?"

"Yessuh." He twisted the one shoulder-strap of his

overalls and Val guessed that his knowledge was something he was either ashamed of or afraid to tell.

"Can you take me there?"

He shook his head. "I ain' a-goin' in here, I ain'!"

"But, Sam, you've got to! Miss 'Chanda is in there. She may be lost. We've got to find her!" Val insisted.

Sam's thin shoulders shook and he slid backward as if to avoid the white boy's reach. "I ain't a-goin' in dere," he repeated stubbornly. "Effen yo' wants to go in—Looky, Mistuh Val, I tells yo' de way an' yo' goes." He brightented at this solution. "Yo' kin take pappy's othah boat; it's downstream, behin' dem willows. Den yo' goes down to de secon' big pile o' willows. Behin' is a li'l bitty bayo,. Yo' goes up dat 'til yo' comes to a fur rack. After 'dat Jeems got a way marked on trees."

With that he turned and ran as if all the terrors of the night were on his trail. There was nothing for Val to do but to follow his directions. And the longer he lingered before setting out the bigger lead Ricky was getting.

He found the canoe behind the willows as Sam had said. Awkwardly he pushed off, hoping that Lucy would pry the whole story out of her son and put Rupert on their track as soon as possible.

The second clump of willows was something of a landmark, a huge matted mass of sucker and branch, the lower tips of the long, frond-like twigs sweeping the murky water. A snake swimming with its head just above the surface wriggled to the bank as Val cut into the small hidden stream Sam had told him of.

Vines and water plants had almost choked this, but there

was a passage through the center. And one tough spike of vegetation which snapped back into his face bore a deep cut from which the sap was still oozing. The small stinging flies and mosquitoes followed and hung over him like a fog of discomfort. His skin was swollen and rough, irritated and itching. And in this green-covered way the heat seemed almost solid. Drops of moisture dripped from forehead and chin, and his hair was plastered tight to his skull.

Frogs leaped from the bank into the water at the sound of his coming. In the shallows near the bank, crawfish scuttled under water-logged leaves and stones at this disturbance of their world. Twice the bayou widened out into a sort of pool where the trees grew out of the muddy water and all sorts of lilies and bulb plants blossomed in riotous confusion.

Once a muskrat waddled into the protection of the bushes. And Val saw something like a small cat drinking. But that faint shadow disappeared noiselessly almost before the water trickled from his upraised paddle.

Clumps of wild rice were the meeting grounds for flocks of screaming birds. A snow-white egret waded solemnly across a mud-rimmed pocket. And once a snake, more dangerous than the swimmer Val had first encountered, betrayed its presence by the flicker of its tongue.

The smell of the steaming mud, the decaying vegetation, and the nameless evils hidden deeper in this water-rotted land was an added torment. The boy shook a large red ant from its grip in the flesh of his hand and wiped the streaming perspiration from his face.

It was then that the canoe floated almost of its own

volition into a dead and distorted strip of country. Black water which gave off an evil odor covered almost half an acre of ground. From this arose the twisted, gaunt gray skeletons of dead oaks. To complete the drear picture a row of rusty-black vultures sat along the broad naked limb of the nearest of these hulks, their red-raw heads upraised as they croaked and sidled up and down.

But the bayou Val was following merely skirted this region, and in a few moments he was again sheltered by flower-grown banks. Then he came upon a structure which must have been the fur rack Sam Two had alluded to, for here was their other boat moored to a convenient willow.

Val fastened the canoe beside it. The turf seemed springy, though here and there it gave way to patches of dark mud. It was on one of these that Ricky had left her mark in the clean-cut outline of the sole of her riding-boot.

With a last desperate slap at a mosquito Val headed inland, following with ease that trail of footprints. Ricky was suffering, too, for her rashness he noted with satisfaction when he discovered a long curly hair fast in the grip of a thorny branch he scraped under.

But the path was not a bad one. And the farther he went the more solid and the dryer it became. Once he passed through a small clearing, man-made, where three or four cotton bushes huddled together forlornly in company with a luxuriant melon patch.

And the melon patch was separated by only a few feet of underbrush from Jeems' domain. In the middle of a clearing was a sturdy platform, reinforced with upright posts and standing about four feet from the surface of the ground. On this was a small cabin constructed of slabs of bark-covered wood. As a dwelling it might be crude, but it had an air of scrupulous neatness. A short distance to one side of the platform was a well-built chicken-run, now inhabited by five hens and a ragged-tailed cock.

The door of the cabin was shut and there were no signs of life save the chickens. But as Val lowered himself painfully onto the second step of the ladder-like stairs leading up to the cabin, he thought he heard someone moving around. Glancing up, he saw Ricky staring down at him, open-mouthed.

"Hello," she called, for one of the few times in her life really astounded.

"Hello," Val answered shortly and shifted his weight to try to relieve the ache in his knee. "Nice day, isn't it?"

11

RALESTONES TO THE RESCUE!

Val! What are you doing here?'' she demanded.

"Following you. Good grief, girl,'' he exploded, "haven't you any better sense than to come into the swamp this way?''

Ricky's mouth lost its laughing curve and her eyes seemed to narrow. She was, by all the signs, distinctly annoyed.

"It's perfectly safe. I knew what I was doing.''

"Yes? Well, I will enjoy hearing Rupert's remarks on that subject when he catches up with us,'' snapped her brother.

"Val!" She lost something of her defiant attitude. He guessed that for all her boasted independence his sister was slightly afraid of Mr. Rupert Ralestone. "Val, he isn't coming, too, is he?"

"He is if he got my message." Val stretched his leg cautiously. The cramp was slowly leaving the muscles and he felt as if he could stand the remaining ache without wincing. "I sent Sam Two back to tell Rupert where his family had eloped to. Frankly, Ricky, this wasn't such a smart trick. You know what Charity said about the swamps. Even the little I've seen of them has given me ideas."

"But there was nothing to it at all," she protested. "Jeems told me just how to get here and I only followed directions."

Val chose to ignore this, being hot, tired, and in no mood for one of those long arguments such as Ricky enjoyed. "By the way, where is Jeems?" He looked about him as if he expected the swamper to materialize out of thin air.

Ricky sat down on the edge of the platform and dangled her booted feet. "Don't know. But he'll be here sooner or later. And I don't feel like going back through the swamp just yet. The flies are awful. And did you see those dreadful vultures on that dead tree? What a place! But the flowers are wonderful and I saw a real live alligator, even if it was a small one." She rubbed her scarf across her forehead. "Whew! It seems hotter here than it does at home."

"This outing was all your idea," Val reminded her. "And we'd better be getting back before Rupert calls out the Marines or the State Troopers or something to track us down."

Ricky pouted. "Not going until I'm ready. And you can't drag me if I dig my heels in."

"I have no desire to be embroiled in such an undignified struggle as you suggest," he told her loftily. "But neither do I yearn to spend the day here. I'm hungry. I wonder if our absent host possesses a larder?"

"If he does, you can't raid it," Ricky answered. "The door's locked, and that lock," she pointed to the bright disk of brass on the solid cabin door, "is a good one. I've already tried a hairpin on it," she added shamelessly.

They sat awhile in silence. A wandering breeze had found its way into the clearing, and with it came the fragrance of flowers blossoming under the sun. The chicken family were pursuing a worm with more energy than Val decided he would have cared to expend in that heat, and a heavily laden bee rested on the lip of a sunflower to brush its legs. Val's eyelids drooped and he found himself thinking dreamily of a hammock under the trees, a pillow, and long hours of lazy dozing. At the same time a corner of his brain was sending forth nagging messages that they should be up and off, back to their own proper world. But he simply did not have the will power to get up and go.

"Nice place," he murmured, looking about with more approbation than he would have granted the clearing some ten minutes earlier.

"Yes," answered Ricky. "It would be nice to live here."

Val was beginning to say something about "no bathtubs"

when a sound aroused them from their lethargy. Someone was coming down the path. Ricky's hand fell upon her brother's shoulder.

"Quick! Up here and behind the house," she urged him.

Not knowing just why he obeyed, Val scrambled up on the tiny platform and scuttled around behind the cabin. Why they should hide thus from Jeems who had given Ricky directions for reaching the place and had asked her to come, was more than he could understand. But he had a faint, uneasy feeling of mistrust, as if they had been caught off guard at a critical moment.

"This the place, Red?" The clipped words sounded clear above the murmurs of life from swamp and woods.

"Yeah. Bum-lookin' joint, ain't it? These guys ain't got no brains; they like to live like this." The contempt of the second speaker was only surpassed by the stridency of his voice.

"What about this boy?" asked the first.

"Dumb kid. Don't know yet who his friends is." There was a satisfied grunt as the speaker sat down on the step Val had so lately vacated. Ricky pressed closer to her brother.

"What about the cabin?"

"He ain't here. And it's locked, see? You'd think he kept the crown jewels there." The tickling scent of a cigarette drifted back to the two in hiding. "Beats me how he slipped away this morning without Pitts catching on. For two cents I'd spring that lock of his—"

"Isn't worth the trouble," replied the other decisively.

148

"These trappers have no money except at the end of the fur season, and then most of them are in debt to the storekeepers."

"Then why—"

"I sometimes wonder," the voice was coldly cutting, "why I continue to employ you, Red. What profit would I find in a cabin like this? I want what he knows, not what he has."

Having thus reduced his henchman to silence, the speaker went on smoothly, as if he were thinking aloud. "With Simpson doing so well in town, we're close to the finish. This swamper must tell us—" His voice trailed away. Except for the creaking of wood when the sitter shifted his position, there was no other sound.

Then Red must have grown restless, for someone stamped up to the platform and rattled the chain on the cabin door aggressively. Val flattened back against the wall. What if the fellow took it into his head to walk around?

"Gonna wait here all day?" demanded Red.

"As it is necessary for me to have a word with him, we will. This waste of time is the product of Pitts' stupidity. I shall remember that. It is entirely needless to use force except as a last resource. Now that this swamper's suspicions are aroused, we may have trouble."

"Yeah? Well, we can handle that. But how do yuh know that this guy has the stuff?"

"I can at least believe the evidence of my own eyes," the other replied with bored contempt. "I came down river alone the night of the storm and saw him on the levee. He has a way of getting into the house all right. I saw him in

149

there. And he doesn't go through any of the doors, either. I must know how he does it.''

"All right, Boss. And what if you do get in? What are we supposed to be lookin' for?''

"What those bright boys up there found a few days ago. That clerk told us that they'd discovered whatever the girl was talking about in the office that day. And we've got to get that before Simpson comes into court with his suit. I'm not going to lose fifty grand.'' The last sentence ended abruptly as if the speaker had snapped his teeth shut upon a word like a dog upon its quarry.

"What does this guy Jeems go to the house for?'' asked Red.

"Who knows? He seems to be hunting something too. But that's not our worry. If it's necessary, we can play ghost also. I've got to get into that house. If I can do it the way this Jeems does, without having to break in—so much the better. We don't want the police ambling around here just now.''

Val stiffened. It didn't require a Sherlock Holmes to get the kernel of truth out of the conversation he had overheard. "Night of the storm,'' "play ghost,'' were enough. So Jeems had been the ghost. And the swamper knew a secret way into the house!

"Wait,'' Ricky's lips formed the words by his ear as Val stirred restlessly. "Someone else is coming.''

"I don't like the set-up in town,'' Red was saying peevishly. "That smooth mouthpiece is asking too darn many questions. He's always asking Simpson about things in the past. If you hadn't got Sim that family history to study, he'd been behind bars a dozen times by now.''

"And he had better study it," commented the other dryly, "because he is going to be word perfect before the case comes to court, if it ever does. There are not going to be any slip-ups in this deal."

" 'Nother thing I don't like," broke in the other, "is this Waverly guy. I don't like his face."

"No? Well, doubtless he would change it if you asked him to. And I do not think it is wise of you to be too critical of plans which were made by deeper thinkers than yourself. Sometimes, Red, you weary me."

There was no reply to that harsh judgment. And now Val could hear what Ricky had heard earlier—a faint swish as of a paddle through water. Again Ricky's lips shaped words he could barely hear.

"Spur of bayou runs along here in back. Someone coming up from there."

"Jeems?"

"Maybe."

"We'd better—" Val motioned toward the front of the cabin. Ricky shook her head. Jeems was to be allowed to meet the intruders unwarned.

"This swamper may be tough," ventured Red.

"We've met hard cases before," answered the other significantly.

Red moved again, as if flexing his muscles.

"One boy, and a small one at that, shouldn't force you to undergo all that preparation," goaded the Boss.

Ricky must get away at once, her brother decided.

Stubbornness or no stubbornness, she must go this time. Why he didn't think of going himself Val never afterwards knew. Perhaps he possessed a spark of the family love of danger, after all, but mostly he clung to his perch because of that last threat. Whoever Jeems was or whatever he had done, he was one and alone. And he might relish another player on his side. But Ricky must go.

He said as much in a fierce whisper, only to have her grin recklessly back at him. In pantomime she gestured that he might try to make her. Val decided that he should have known the result of his efforts. Ricky was a Ralestone, too. And short of throwing her off the platform and so unmasking themselves completely, he could not move her against her will.

"No," she whispered. "They're planning trouble for Jeems. He'll probably need us."

"Well," Val cautioned her, "if it gets too tough, you've got to promise to cut downstream for help. We'll be able to use it."

She nodded. "It's a promise. But we've got to stand by Jeems if he needs us."

"*If* he does—" Val was still suspicious. "He may fall in with their suggestions."

Ricky shook her head. "He isn't that kind. I don't care if he *has* been playing ghost."

Someone was walking along the path among the bushes bordering the back of the clearing. Although they could hear no sound, they could mark the passing of a body by the swish of the foliage. Val lay, face down, on the platform and reached for a stick of wood lying on the ground below. Somehow he did not like to think of being caught empty-handed when the excitement began.

"Hello." It was Red, suddenly genial. The Ralestones could almost feel the radiance of the smile which must have split his face.

"Whatta yo' doin' heah?" That was Jeems, and his demand was sharply hostile.

"Now, bub, don't get us wrong." That was Red, still genial. "I know my pal sorta flew off his base this mornin'. But it was all in fun, see? So we kinda wanted yuh to stick around till he came and not do the run-out on us. And now the Boss has come down here so we can talk business all friendly like."

"Shut up, Red!" Having so bottled his companion's flow of words, the other spoke directly to Jeems. "My men made a mistake. All right. That's over and done with; they'll get theirs. Now let's get down to business. What do you know about that big plantation up river, the one called 'Pirate's Haven'?"

"Nothin'." Jeems' answer was clear. The hostility was gone from his voice; nothing remained but an even tonelessness.

"Come now, I know you have reason to be hot. But this is business. I'll make it worth your while—"

"Nothin'," answered Jeems as concisely as before.

"You can't expect us to believe that. I followed you one night."

"Yo' did?" The challenge was unmistakable.

"I did. So you see I know something of you. Something

153

which even the present owner does not. Say the ghost in the hall, for example.''

There was the sound of a deeply drawn breath.

''So you see it is to your advantage to listen to us,'' continued the Boss smoothly.

''What do yo' want?''

Val knew disappointment at that question. Would Jeems surrender as easily as that?

''Just an explanation of how you get into the house unseen.''

''Yo'll nevah know!'' The swamper's reply came swift and clear.

''No? Well, I'd think twice before I held to that answer if I were you,'' purred the other softly. ''A word to the Ralestones about those nightly waiks of yours—''

''Won't give yo' what yo' want,'' replied Jeems shrewdly.

''I see. Perhaps I have been using the wrong approach,'' observed the Boss composedly. ''You work for a living, don't you?''

''Yes.''

''Then you know the value of money. What is your price? Come on, we won't haggle.''

The Boss' impatience colored his tone. ''How much do you want for this information?''

''Nothin'!''

''Nothing?''

''Ah ain't said nothin' an' Ah ain't a-goin' to say nothin'. An' yo' bettah be a-gittin' offen this heah land of mine afo'—''

"Before what, swamper?" Red was taking a hand in the game.

"Yo' can't fright'n me with that gun," came calmly enough from Jeems. "Yo' ain't a-goin' to risk shootin'—"

"There ain't no witnesses here, kid. And there ain't no law back in these swamps. Yuh're gonna tell the Boss what he wants to know an' yuh're gonna spill it quick, see? I know some ways of making guys squeal—"

At that suggestion Val's fingers tightened on his club and Ricky choked back a cry as her brother crept toward the corner of the cabin. Their melodrama was fast taking on the color of tragedy.

"So yuh better speak up." Red was still encouraging Jeems.

There was no immediate answer from the swamper, but Ricky touched Val's arm and nodded toward the bushes. She had decided that it was time for her to leave. He agreed eagerly. She dropped lightly to the ground and he watched her crawl away unnoticed by those in front who were so intent upon the baiting of their quarry.

"Three minutes, swamper!"

Ricky was gone, free from whatever might develop. Val edged forward and for the first time peered around the corner of the cabin. The two assailants were still only voices, but he could see Jeems. The swamper's face was bruised and there was a smear of dried blood across one cheek as if he had already been roughly handled. But he stood at ease, facing the cabin. His hands were hanging loosely at his sides and he was seemingly unconcerned by what confronted him. Suddenly his eyes flickered to the

155

bushes at one side. Had Ricky betrayed herself, Val wondered breathlessly.

Clear now of the cabin, Val wriggled his way around the platform. In a minute he would be able to see the Boss and Red. He gripped the club.

Then Jeems stared straight into his face. But the swamper gave no sign of seeing Val. And that, to the boy's mind, was the greatest feat of all that afternoon. For Val knew that if he had been in Jeems' place he would have betrayed them both in his surprise.

The others were at last visible, their backs to Val. Nervously he sized them up. The Boss was tall and thin, but his movements suggested possession of wiry strength. Red, his brick-colored hair making him easy to identify, was shorter and thick across the shoulders, but his waistline was also thick and the boy thought that his wind was bad. Of the two, the Boss was the more dangerous. Red might lose his head in a sudden attack, but not the Boss. Val decided to tackle the latter.

Slowly he got from his knees to his feet. After the first quick glance, Jeems hadn't looked at him, but Val knew that the swamper was ready and waiting to take advantage of any diversion he might make.

"Three minutes are up, swamper. So yuh've decided to be tough, eh?"

"Whatta yo' wanna know?" Jeems' question held their attention.

"We have told you several times," answered the Boss, his temper beginning to fray visibly. "What is the trick of getting into that house?"

"Well," Jeems raised his hand to rub his ear, "yo' turn to the left—"

So he agreed with the listener. Val was to take the Boss on his left. He gathered his feet under him for the leap which he hoped would land him full upon the invader.

"Yes?" prompted the man impatiently as Jeems hesitated. At that moment Val sprang.

But his game leg betrayed him again. Instead of landing cleanly upon the other, he came down draggingly across the Boss's shoulders. The gun roared and then the attacked man lashed back a vicious blow which split the skin over Val's cheekbone.

For the next three minutes Val was more than occupied. His opponent was a dirty fighter, and when he had recovered from his surprise he was more than the boy could handle. Val's club was twisted out of his hands, and he found himself fighting wildly to keep the man's clawing fingers from his eyes. They were both rolling on the ground, flailing out at each other. Twice Val tasted his own blood when one of the enemy's vicious jabs glanced along his face. Either blow would have finished Val had it landed clean.

Then in a sudden turn the Boss caught him in a deadly body-lock which left him half-stunned and panting, at his mercy. And there was no mercy in the man. When Val looked up into that flushed, snarling face, he knew that he was as hopeless as a trapped animal. The man could—and would—finish him at his leisure.

"This way, Rupert! Sam!" the cry reached even Val's dulled ears.

The man above him stirred. The boy saw the blood-lust fade from his eyes and apprehension take its place. He got to his feet, launching a last bruising kick at Val's ribs before he limped across the clearing. On his way he hauled Red to his feet. They were going, not toward the path from the bayou, but around the house on the trail that Jeems had followed. Val struggled up and looked around. The turf was torn and gouged. In the dust lay his club and Red's revolver.

And by the steps lay something else, a slight brown figure. Painfully the boy got to his feet and lurched across to Jeems.

12

THE RALESTONES BRING HOME
A RELUCTANT GUEST

The swamper was lying on his back, his eyes closed. From a great purple welt across his forehead blood oozed sluggishly. When Val touched him he moaned faintly.

"Val! Are you hurt? What's the matter?" Ricky was upon them like a whirlwind out of the bush.

"Jeems stopped a nasty one," her brother panted.

"Is he——" She dropped down in the dust beside them.

"He's knocked out, and he'll have a bad headache for some time, but I don't think it's any worse than that."

Ricky had pulled out a microscopic bit of handkerchief and was dabbing at the blood in an amateurish way. Jeems moaned and turned his head as if to get away from her ministrations.

"Where's Rupert—and Sam?" Val looked toward the path. "They were with you, weren't they?"

Ricky shook her head. "No. That was just what you call creating a diversion. For all I know, they're busy at home."

Her brother straightened. "Then we've got to get out of here—fast. Those two left because they were rattled, but when they have had a chance to cool off they'll be back."

"What about Jeems?"

"Take him with us, of course. We won't be able to manage the canoe. But you brought the outboard, so we'll go in that and tow the canoe. We ought to have something to cover his head." Val regarded the bleeding wound doubtfully.

Without answering, Ricky leaned forward and began systematically going through Jeems' pockets. In the second she found a key. Val took it from her and hobbled up the cabin steps. For a wonder, he thought thankfully, the key was the right one. The lock clicked and he went in.

Like the clearing, the interior of the one-room shack was neat, a place for everything and everything in its place. Under the window in the far wall was a small chest of some dark polished wood. Save for its size, it was not unlike the chests the Ralestones had found in their storeroom. Opposite it was a wooden cot, the covers smoothly spread. A stool, a blackened cook stove, and a solid table with an oil lamp were the extent of the furnishings. Lines of traps hung on the walls, along with the wooden boards for the stretching of drying skins, and there was a half-finished grass basket lying on top of the chest.

Val hefted a stoneware jug. They had no time to hunt for a spring. And if this contained water, they would need it. At the resulting gurgle from within, he set it by the door and returned to rob the cot of pillow and the single coarse but clean sheet.

Ricky tore the sheet and made a creditable job of washing and bandaging the ugly bruise. Jeems drank greedily when they offered him water but he did not seem to recognize them. In answer to Ricky's question of how he felt, he muttered something in the swamp French of the Cajuns. But he was uneasy until Val locked the cabin door and put the key in his hand.

"How are we going to get him to the boat?" asked Ricky suddenly.

"Carry him."

"But, Val—" for the first time she looked at her brother as if she really saw him— "Val, you're hurt!"

"Just a little stiff," he hastened to assure her. "Our late visitors play rather rough. We'll manage all right. I'll take his shoulders and you his feet."

They wavered drunkenly along the path. Twice Val stumbled and regained his balance just in time. Ricky had laid the pillow across their burden's feet, declaring that she would need it when they got to the boat. Val passed the point of aching misery—when he thought that he could not shuffle forward another step—and now he came into what he had heard called "second wind." By fixing his eyes on a tree or a bush a step or two ahead and concentrating only upon passing that one, and then that, and that, he got through without disgracing himself.

At the bayou at last, they wriggled Jeems awkwardly into the boat. Val had no doubt that a woodsman might have done the whole job better in much less time and without a tenth of the effort they had expended. But all he ever wondered afterward was how they ever did it at all.

It was when Ricky had made their passenger as comfortable as she could in the bottom of the boat, steadying his head across her knees, that her brother partially relaxed.

"Val, you run the engine," she said without looking up.

He dragged himself toward the stern of the boat, remembering too late, when he had cast off, that he had not taken the canoe in tow. The engine coughed, sputtered, and then settled down to a steady *putt-putt*. They were off.

"Val, do you—do you think he is badly hurt?"

He dared not look down; it required all his powers of concentration on what lay before them to keep his hand steady.

"No. We'll get a doctor when we get back. He'll come around again in no time—Jeems, I mean."

But would he? Head injuries were sometimes more serious than they seemed, Val remembered dismally.

It was not until they came out into the main bayou that Jeems roused again. He looked up at Ricky in a sort of dull surprise, and then his gaze shifted to Val.

"What—"

"We won the war," Val tried to grin, an operation

162

which tore his mask of dried blood, "thanks to Ricky. And now we're going home."

At that, Jeems made a violent effort to sit up.

"*Non!*" his English deserted him and he broke into impassioned French.

"Yes," Val replied firmly as Ricky pushed the swamper down. "Of course you're coming with us. You've had a nasty knock on the head that needs attention."

"Ah'm not a-goin' to no hospital!" His eyes burned into Val's.

"Certainly not!" cried Ricky. "You're bound for our guest-room. Now keep quiet. We'll be there soon."

"Ah ain't a-goin'," he declared mutinously.

"Don't be silly," Ricky scolded him; "we're taking you. Does Val have to come and hold you down?"

"Ah can't!" His eyes flickered from Val's face to hers. There was something more than independence behind that firm refusal. "Ah ain't a-goin' theah."

"Why not?"

He seemed to shrink from her. "It ain't fitten," he murmured.

"How perfectly silly," laughed Ricky. But Val thought that he understood.

"Because of the secret you know?" he asked quietly.

The pallor beneath Jeems' heavy tan vanished in a flush of slow-burning red. "Ah reckon so," he muttered, but he met Val's eyes squarely.

"Let's leave all explanations until later," Val suggested.

"Ah played haunt!" the confession came out of the swamper in a rush.

"Then you *were* my faceless ghost?"

Jeems tried to nod and the action printed a frown of pain between his eyes.

"Why? Didn't you want us to live there?" asked Ricky gently.

"Ah was huntin'—"

"What for?"

The frown became one of puzzlement. "Ah don't know—" His voice trailed off into a thin whisper as his eyes closed wearily. Val signaled Ricky to keep quiet.

"Ahoy there!" Along the bank toward them came Rupert and after him Sam. Beyond them lay the Ralestone landing. Val headed inshore.

"Just what does this mean—Val! Has there been an accident?" The irritation in Rupert's voice became hot concern.

"An intended one," his brother replied. "We've got the real victim here with us."

They tied up to the landing and Sam came down to hand out Jeems who apparently had lapsed into unconsciousness again.

"You'd better call a doctor," Val told Rupert. "Jeems has a head wound."

But Rupert had already taken charge of affairs with an efficiency which left Val humbly grateful. The boy didn't even move to leave the boat. It was better just to sit and watch other people scurry about. Sam had started for the house, carrying Jeems as if the long-legged swamper was the same age and size as his own small son. Ricky dashed on ahead to warn Lucy. Rupert had Sam Two by the collar and was giving him instructions for catching Dr. LeFrode, who was probably making his morning rounds and might be found at the sugar-mill where one of the feeders had injured his hand. Sam Two's sister had seen the doctor on his way there a scant ten minutes earlier.

Val watched all this activity dreamily. Everything would be all right now that Rupert was in charge. He could relax—

"Now," his brother turned upon Val, "just what did— What's the matter with you?"

"Tired, I guess," Val said ruefully. But Rupert was already in the boat, getting the younger boy to his unsteady feet.

"Can you make it to the house?" he asked anxiously.

"Sure. Just give me an arm till I get on the landing."

But when Val had crawled up on the levee he did not feel at all like walking to the house. Then Rupert's arm was about his thin shoulders and he thought that he could make it if he really tried.

The garden path seemed miles long, and it was not until Val had the soft cushions of the hall couch under him that he felt able to tell his story. But at that moment the short, stout doctor came through the door in a rush. Sam Two had led him to believe that half the household had been murdered. At first Dr. LeFrode started toward Val, until in alarm the boy swung his feet to the floor and sat up, waving the man to the stairway where Ricky hovered to act as guide.

Then Val was alone, even Sam Two having edged upstairs to share in the excitement. The boy sank back on his pillows and wondered where their late assailants were now, and why they had been so determined to learn Jeems' secret. As Ricky had said once before, the Ralestones seemed to have been handed a gigantic tangle without ends, only middle sections, and had been told to unravel it.

Boot heels clicked on the stone flooring. Val turned his head cautiously and tried not to wince. Rupert was coming in with a bowl of water, from which steam still arose. Across his arm lay a towel and in his other hand was their small first-aid kit.

"Suppose we do a little patching," he suggested. "Your face at present is not all it might be. What did you and your swamp friend do—run into a mowing machine?" He swabbed delicately at the cut the Boss had opened across Val's cheek-bone, and at another by his mouth.

"I thought it might be that for a moment—a mowing machine, I mean. No, we just met a couple of gentlemen— enterprising fellows who wanted to see more of this commodious mansion of ours—" Val's words faded into a sharp hiss as Rupert applied iodine with a liberal hand. "They seemed to think that Jeems knew a lot about Pirate's Haven and they were going to persuade him to tell all. Only it didn't turn out the way they had planned."

"Due to you?" Rupert eyed his brother intently. The boy's face was swollen almost out of recognition and he didn't like this sudden talkativeness.

"Due partly to me, but mostly to Ricky. She—ah— created the necessary diversion. I had sort of lost interest at the time. I know so little about gouging and biting in clinches."

"Dirty fighters?"

"Well, soiled anyway. But if the Boss isn't nursing a cracked wrist, it isn't my fault. I don't know what Jeems did to Red, but he, too, departed in a damaged condition. Do you have to do that?" Val demanded testily, squirming as Rupert ran his hands lightly over the boy's shoulders and down his ribs, touching every bruise to tingling life.

"Just seeing the extent of the damage," he explained.

"You don't have to see, I can feel!" Val snapped pettishly.

Rupert got to his feet. "Come on."

"Where?"

"Oh, a hot bath and then bed. You'll be taking an interest in life again about this time tomorrow. I think LeFrode had better see you too."

"No," Val objected. "I'm not a child."

Rupert grinned. "If you'd rather I carried you—"

There was no opposing Rupert when he was in that mood, as his brother well knew. Val got up slowly.

The program that Rupert had outlined was faithfully carried out. Half an hour later Val found himself between sheets, blinking at the ceiling drowsily. When two cracks overhead wavered together of their own accord, his eyes closed.

"—still sleeping?" whispered someone at his side much later.

"Yes, best thing for him."

"Was he badly hurt?"

"No, just banged around more than was good for him."

Val opened his eyes. It must have been close to dusk,

for the sunlight was red across the bedclothes. Rupert stood by the window and Ricky was in the doorway, a tray of covered dishes in her hands.

"Hello!" Val sat up, grimacing at the twinge of pain across his back. "What day is this?"

Rupert laughed. "Still Tuesday."

"How's Jeems?"

"Doing very well. I've had to have Rupert in to frighten him into staying in bed," Ricky said. "The doctor thinks he ought to be there a couple of days at least. But Jeems doesn't agree with him. Between keeping Jeems in bed and keeping Rupert out of the swamp I've had a full day."

Rupert sat down on the foot of the bed. "You'd know this Boss and Red again, wouldn't you?"

"Of course."

"Then you'll probably have a chance to identify them." There was a grim look about Rupert's jaw. "Ricky's told me all that you overheard. I don't know what it means but I've heard enough for me to get in touch with LeFleur. He'll be out tomorrow morning. And once we get something to work on—"

"I'm beginning to feel sorry for our swamp visitors," Val interrupted.

"They'll be sorry," hinted Rupert darkly. "How about you, Val, beginning to feel hungry?"

"Now that you mention it, I *am* discovering a rather hollow ache in my center section. Supper ready?"

"Half an hour. I'll bring you up a tray—" began Ricky. But Val had thrown back the sheet and was sitting on the side of the bed. "Oh, no, you don't! I'm not an invalid yet."

Ricky glanced at Rupert and then left. Val reached for his shirt defiantly. But his brother raised no objection. The painful stiffness Val had felt at first wore off and he was able to move without feeling as if each muscle were tied in cramping knots.

"May I pay Jeems a visit?" he asked as they went out into the hall. Rupert nodded toward a door across the corridor.

"In there. He's a stubborn piece of goods. Reminds me of you at times. If he'd ever get rid of that scowl of his, he'd be even more like you. He warms to Ricky, but you'd think I was a Chinese torturer the way he acts when I go in." There was a shade of irritation in Rupert's voice.

"Maybe he's afraid of you."

"But what for?" Rupert stared at the boy in open surprise.

"Well, you do have rather a commanding air at times," Val countered. If Ricky had told Rupert nothing of Jeems' confession, he wasn't going to.

"So that's what you really think of me!" observed Rupert. "Go reason with that wildcat if you want to. I'm beginning to believe that you are two of a kind." He turned abruptly down the hall.

Val opened the door of the bedroom. The sunlight was fading fast and already the corners of the large room were filled with the gray of dusk. But light from the windows swept full across the bed and its occupant. Val hobbled stiffly toward it.

"Hello." The brown face on the pillow did not change expression as Val greeted the swamper. "How do you feel now?"

"Bettah," Jeems answered shortly. "Ah'm good but they won't le' me up."

"The Doc says you're in for a couple of days," Val told him.

Somehow Jeems looked smaller, shrunken, as he lay in that oversized bed. And he had lost that air of indolent arrogance which had made him seem so independent in their swamp and garden meetings. It was as if Val were looking down upon a younger and less confident edition of the swamper he had known.

"What does he think?" There was urgency in that question.

"Who's he?"

"Yo' brothah."

"Rupert? Why, he's glad to have you here," Val answered.

"Does he know 'bout—"

Val shook his head.

"Tell him!" ordered the swamper. "Ah ain't a-goin' to say undah his roof lessen he knows. 'Tain't fitten."

At this clean-cut statement of the laws of hospitality, Val nodded. "All right. I'll tell him. But what were you after here, Jeems? I'll have to tell him that, too, you know. Was it the Civil War treasure?"

Jeems turned his head slowly. "No." Again the puzzled frown twisted his straight, finely marked brows. "What do

Ah want wi' treasure? Ah don't know what Ah was lookin' fo'. Mah grandpappy—"

"Val, supper's ready," came Rupert's voice from the hall.

Val half turned to go. "I've got to go now. But I'll be back later," he promised.

"Yo'll tell him?" Jeems stabbed a finger at the door.

"Yes; after supper. I promise."

With a little sigh Jeems relaxed and burrowed down into the softness of the pillow. "Ah'll be awaitin'," he said.

13

ON SUCH A NIGHT AS THIS—

It had been one of those dull, weepy days when a sullen drizzle clouded sky and earth. In consequence, the walls and floors of Pirate's Haven seemed to exude chill. Rupert built a fire in the hall fireplace, but none of the family could say that it was a successful one. It made a nice show of leaping flame accompanied by fancy lighting effects but gave forth absolutely no heat.

"Val?"

The boy started guiltily and thrust his notebook under the couch cushion as Charity came in. Tiny drops of rain were strung along the hairs which had blown free of her rain-cape hood like steel beads along a golden wire.

"Yes? Don't come here expecting to get warm," he warned her bitterly. "We are very willing but the fire is weak. Looks pretty, doesn't it?" He kicked at a charred end on the hearth. "Well, that's all it's good for!"

"Val, what sort of a mess have you and Jeems jumped into?" she asked as she handed him her dripping cape.

"Oh, just a general sort of mess," he answered lightly. "Jeems had callers who forgot their manners. So Ricky and I breezed in and brought the party to a sudden end—"

"As I can see by your black eye," she commented. "But what has Jeems been up to?"

Val was suddenly very busy holding her cape before that mockery of a blaze.

"Why don't you ask him that?"

"Because I'm asking you. Rupert came over last night and sat on my gallery making very roundabout inquiries concerning Jeems. I pried out of him the details of your swamp battle. But I want to know now just what Jeems has been doing. Your brother is so vague—"

"Rupert has the gift of being exasperatingly uncommunicative," his brother told her. "The story, so far as I know, is short and simple. Jeems knows a secret way into this house. In addition, his grandfather told him that the fortune of the house of Jeems is concealed here—having been very hazy in his description of the nature of said fortune. Consequently, grandson has been playing haunt up and down our halls trying to find it.

"His story is as full of holes as a sieve but somehow one can't help believing it. He has explained that he has the secret of the outside entrance only, and not the one

173

opening from the inside. In the meantime he is in bed—
guarded from intrusion by Ricky and Lucy with the same
care as if he were the crown jewels. So matters rest at
present.''

''Neatly put.'' She dropped down on the couch. ''By
the way, do you realize that you have ruined your face for
my uses?''

Val fingered the crisscrossing tape on his cheek. ''This
is only temporary.''

''I certainly hope so. That nust have been some battle.''

''One of our better efforts.'' He coughed in mock
modesty. ''Ricky saved the day with alarms and excur-
sions without. Rupert probably told you that.''

''Yes, he can be persuaded to talk at times. Is he always
so silent?''

''Nowadays, yes,'' he answered slowly. ''But when
we were younger—You know,'' Val turned toward her
suddenly, his brown face serious to a degree, ''it isn't fair
to separate the members of a family. To put one here and one
there and the third somewhere else. I was twelve when
Father died, and Ricky was eleven. They sent her off to
Great-aunt Rogers because Uncle Fleming, who took me,
didn't care for a girl—''

''And Rupert?''

''Rupert—well, he was grown, he could arrange his
own life; so he just went away. We got a letter now and
then, or a post-card. There was money enough to send us
to expensive schools and dress us well. It was two years
before I really saw Ricky again. You can't call short visits
on Sunday afternoons seeing anyone.

"Then Uncle Fleming died and I was simply parked at Great-aunt Rogers'. She"—Val was remembering things, a bitter look about his mouth—"didn't care for boys. In September I was sent to a military academy. I needed discipline, it seemed. And Ricky was sent to Miss Somebody's-on-the-Hudson. Rupert was in China then. I got a letter from him that fall. He was about to join some expedition heading into the Gobi.

"Ricky came down to the Christmas hop at the academy, then Aunt Rogers took her abroad. She went to school in Switzerland a year. I passed from school to summer camp and then back to school. Ricky sent me some carvings for Christmas—they arrived three days late."

He stared up at the stone mantel. "Kids feel things a lot more than they're given credit for. Ricky sent me a letter with some tear stains between the lines when Aunt Rogers decided to stay another year. And that was the year I earned the reputation of being a 'hard case.'

"Then Ricky cabled me that she was coming home. I walked out of school the same morning. I didn't even tell anyone where I was going. Because I had money enough, I thought I would fly. And that, dear lady, is the end of this very sad tale." He grinned one-sidedly down at her.

"It was then that—that—"

"I was smashed up? Yes. And Rupert came home without warning to find things very messy. I was in the hospital when I should have been in some corrective institution, as Aunt Rogers so often told me during those days. Ricky was also in disgrace for speaking her mind, as she does now and then. To make it even more interesting, our

175

guardian had been amusing himself by buying oil stock with our capital. Unfortunately, oil did not exist in the wells we owned. Yes, Rupert had every right to be anything but pleased with the affairs of the Ralestones.

"He swept us off here where we are still under observation, I believe."

"Then you don't like it here?"

"Like it? Madam, 'like' is a very pallid word. What if you were offered everything you ever wished for, all tied up in pink ribbons and laid on your door-step? What would your reaction be?"

"So," she was staring into the fire, "that's the way of it?"

"Yes. Or it would be if—" He stooped to reach for another piece of wood. The fire was threatening to die again.

"What is the flaw in the masterpiece?" she asked quietly.

"Rupert. He's changed. In the old days he was one of us; how he's a stranger. We're amusing to have around, someone to look after, but I have a feeling that to him we don't really exist. We aren't real—" Val floundered trying to express that strange, walled-off emotion which so often held him in this grown-up brother's presence. "Things like this 'Bluebeard's Chamber' of his—that isn't like the Rupert we knew."

"Did you ever think that he might be shy, too?" she asked. "He left two children and came home to find two distrustful adults. Give him his chance—"

"Charity!" Ricky ran lightly downstairs. "Why didn't Val tell me you had come?"

"I just dropped in to inquire concerning your patient."

"He's better-tempered than Val," declared Ricky shamelessly. "You'll stay to dinner of course. We're having some sort of crab dish that Lucy seems to think her best effort. Rupert will be back by then, I'm sure; he's out somewhere with Sam. There's been some trouble about trespassers on the swamp lands. Goodness, won't this rain ever stop?"

As if in answer to her question, there came a great gust of wind and rain against the door, a blast which shook the oak, thick and solid as it was. And then came the thunder of the knocker which Letty-Lou had polished into shining life only the day before.

Val opened the door to find Mr. Creighton and Mr. Holmes huddled on the mat. They came in with an eagerness which was only surpassed by Satan, wet and displaying cold anger towards his mistress, whom he passed with a disdainful flirt of his tail as he headed for that deceptive fire.

"You, again," observed Charity resignedly as Sam Two was summoned and sent away again draped with wet coats and drenched hats.

"Man"—Holmes argued with Satan for the possession of the hearthstone—"when it rains in this country, it rains. A branch of your creek down there is almost over the road—"

"Bayou, not creek," corrected Charity acidly. Lately she had shown a marked preference for Holmes' absence rather than his company.

177

"I stand corrected," he laughed; "a branch of your bayou."

"If you found it so unpleasant, why did you—" began Charity, and then she flushed as if she had suddenly realized that that speech was too rude even for her recent attitude.

"Why did we come?" Holmes' crooked eyebrow slid upward as his face registered mock reproof. "My, my, what a warm welcome, my dear." He shook his head and Charity laughed in spite of herself.

"Don't mind my bearishness," she made half apology. "You know what pleasant moods I fall into while working. And this rain is depressing."

"But Miss Biglow is right." Creighton smiled his rare, shy smile. Brusque and impatient as he was when on business bent, he was awkwardly uncomfortable in ordinary company. The man, Val sometimes thought privately, lived, ate, slept books. Save when they were the subject of conversation, he was as out of his element as a coal-miner at the ballet. "We should explain the reason for this—this rather abrupt call." He fingered his brief-case, which he still clutched, nervously.

"Down to business already." Holmes seated himself on the arm of Ricky's chair. "Very well, out with it."

Creighton smiled again, laid the case across his knees, and looked straight at Ricky. For some reason he talked to her, as if she above all others must be firmly convinced of the importance of his mission.

"It is a very queer story, Miss Ralestone, a very queer—"

"Said the mariner to the wedding guest." Holmes snapped

his fingers at Satan, who contemptuously ignored him. "Or am I thinking of the Whiting who talked to the Snail?"

"Perhaps I had better begin at the beginnin," continued Creighton, frowning at Holmes who refused to be so suppressed.

"Why be so dramatic about it, old man? It's very simple, Miss Ricky. Creighton has lost an author and he wants you to help find him."

When Ricky's eyes involuntarily swept about the room, Val joined in the laughter. "No, it isn't as easy as all that, I'm afraid." Creighton had lost his nervous shyness. "But what Holmes says is true. I have lost an author and do hope that you can help me locate the missing gentleman—or lady. Two months ago an agent sent a manuscript to our office for reading. It wasn't complete, but he thought it was well worth our attention. It was.

"Although there were only five chapters finished, the rest being but symopsis and elaborated scenes, we knew that we had something—something big. We delayed reporting upon it until Mr. Brewster—our senior partner—returned from Europe. Mr. Brewster has the final decision on all manuscripts; he was as well pleased with this offering as we were. Frankly, we saw possibilities of another great success such as those other long historical novels which have been so popular during the past few years.

"Queerly enough, the author's name was not upon the papers sent us by the agent—that is, his proper name; there was a pen-name. And when we applied to Mr. Lever, the agent, we received a most unpleasant shock. The author's real name, which had been given in the covering letter mailed with the manuscript to Mr. Lever, had most strangely disappeared, due to some carelessness in his office.

"Now we have an extremely promising book and no author—"

"What I can't understand," cut in Holmes, "is the modesty of the author. Why hasn't he written to Lever?"

"That is the most unfortunate part of the whole affair." Mr. Creighton shook his head. "Lever recalled that the chap had said in the letter that if Lever found the manuscript unsalable he should destroy it, as the writer was moving about and had no permanent address. The fellow added that if he didn't hear from Lever he would assume that it was not acceptable. Lever wrote to the address given in the letter to acknowledge receipt, but that was all."

"Mysterious," Val commented, interested in spite of himself.

"Just so. Lever deduced from the tone of the letter that the writer was very uncertain of his own powers and hesitated to submit his manuscript. And yet, what we have is a very fine piece of work, far beyond the ability of the average beginner. The author must have written other things.

"The novel is historical, with a New Orleans setting. Its treatment is so detailed that only one who had lived here or had close connections with this country could have produced it. Mr. Brewster, knowing that I was about to travel south, asked me to see if I could discover our missing author through his material. So far I have failed; our man

180

is unknown to any of the writers of the city or to any of those interested in literary matters.

"Yet he knows New Orleans and its history as few do today except those of old family who have been born and bred here. Dr. Hanly Richardson of Tulane University has assured me that much of the material used is authentic— historically correct to the last detail. And it was Dr. Richardson who suggested that several of the scenes must have actually occurred, becoming with the passing of time part of the tradition of some aristocratic family.

"The period of the story is that time of transition when Louisiana passed from Spain to France and then under the control of the United States. It covers the years immediately precediing the Battle of New Orleans. Unfortunately, those were years of disturbance and change. Events which might have been the talk of the town, and so have found description in gossipy memoirs, were swallowed by happenings of national importance. It is, I believe, in intimate family records only that I can find the clue I seek."

"Which scenes"—Richy's eyes shone in the firelight— "are those Dr. Richardson believes real?"

"Well, he was very certain that the duel of the twin brothers must have occurred— Why, Mr. Ralestone," he interrupted himself as the stick Val was about to place on the fire fell from his hands and rolled across the floor. "Mr. Ralestone, what is the matter?"

Across his shoulder Ricky signaled her brother. And above her head Val saw Holmes' eyes narrow shrewdly.

"Nothing. I'm sorry I was so clumsy." Val stooped hurriedly to hide his confusion.

"A duel between twin brothers." Ricky twisted one of the buttons which marched down the front of her sport dress. "That sounds exciting."

"They fought at midnight"—Creighton was enthralled by the story he was telling—"and one was left for dead. The scene is handled with restraint and yet you'd think that the writer had been an eye-witness. Now if such a thing ever did happen, there would have been a certain amount of talk afterwards—"

Charity nodded. "The slaves would have spread the news," she agreed, "and the person who found the wounded twin."

Val kept his eyes upon the hearthstone. There was no stain there, but his vivid imagination painted the gray as red as it had been that cold night when the slave woman had come to find her master lying there, her brother's sword across his body. Someone had used the story of the missing Ralestone. But who today knew that the story except themselves, Charity, LeFleur, and some of the blacks.

"And you think that some mention of such an event might be found in the papers of the family concerned?" asked Ricky. She was leaning forward in her chair, her lips parted eagerly.

"Or in those of some other family covering the same period," Creighton added. "I realize that this is an impertinence on my part, but I wonder if such mention might not be found among the records of your own house. From what I have seen and heard, your family was very prominent in the city affairs of that time—"

Ricky stood up. "There is no need to ask, Mr. Creighton. My brother and I will be most willing to help you. Unfortunately, Rupert is very much immersed in a business matter just now, but Val and I will go through the papers we have."

Val choked down the protest that was on his lips just in time to nod agreement. For some reason Ricky wanted to keep the secret. Very well, he would play her game. At least he would until he knew what lay behind her desire for silence.

"That is most kind." Creighton was beaming upon both of them. "I cannot tell you how much I appreciate your coöperation in this matter—"

"Not at all," answered Ricky with that deceptive softness in her voice which masked her rising temper. "We are only too grateful to be allowed to share a secret."

And then her brother guessed that she did not mean Creighton's secret but some other. She crossed the room and rang the bell for Letty-Lou to bring coffee. Something triumphant in her step added to Val's suspicion. Like the Englishman of Kipling's poem, Ricky was most to be feared when she grew polite. He turned in time to see her wink at Charity.

Rupert came in just then, wet and thoroughly out of sorts, full of the evidences he had discovered on Ralestone lands bordering the swamp that strangers had been camping there. Their guests all stayed to supper, lingering long about the table to discuss Rupert's find, so that Val did not get a chance to be alone with Ricky to demand an explanation. And for some reason she seemed to be adroitly

183

avoiding him. He did have her almost cornered in the upper hall when Letty-Lou came up behind him and plucked at his sleeve.

"Mistuh Val," she said, "that Jeems boy wants to see yo'all."

"Brother Jeems!" Val exploded, his eyes on Ricky's back. But he stepped into the bedroom where the swamper was still imprisoned by Lucy's orders.

The boy was propped up on his pillows, looking out of the window. His body was tense. At the sound of Val's step he turned his bandaged head.

"Can't yo' git me outa heah?" he demanded.

"Why?"

"The watah's up!" His eyes were upon the water-filled darkness of the garden.

"But that's all right," the other assured him. "Sam says that it won't reach the top of the levee. At the worst, only the lower part of the garden will be flooded."

Jeems glanced at Val over his shoulder and then without a word he edged toward the side of the bed and tried to stand. But with a muffled gasp he sank back again, pale and weak. Awkwardly Val forced him back against his pillows.

"It's all right," he assured him again.

But in answer the swamper shook his head violently, "It ain't all right in the swamp."

In a flash Val caught his meaning. Swampers lived on house-boats for the most part, and the boats will outride all but unusual floods. But Jeems' cabin was built on land,

land none too stable even in dry weather. The swamp boy touched Val's hand.

"It ain't safe. Two of them piles is rotted. If the watah gits that far, they'll go."

"You mean the piles holding up your cabin platform?', Val asked.

He nodded. For a second Val caught a glimpse of forlorn loneliness beneath the sullen mask Jeems habitually wore.

"But there's nothing you can do now—"

"It ain't the cabin. Ah gotta git the chest—"

"The one in the cabin?"

His black eyes were fixed upon Val's, and then they swerved and rested upon the wall behind the young Ralestone.

"Ah gotta git the chest," he repeated simply.

And Val knew that he would. He would get out of bed and go into the swamp after that treasure of his. Which left only one thing for Val to do.

"I'll get the chest, Jeems. Let me have your key to the cabin. I'll take the outboard motor and be back before I'm missed."

"Yo' don't know the swamp—"

"I know how to find the cabin. Where's the key?"

"In theah," he pointed to the highboy.

Val's fingers closed about the bit of metal.

"Mistuh," Jeems straightened, "Ah won't forgit this."

Val glanced toward the downpour without.

"Neither will I, in all probability," he said dryly as he went out.

It had been on just such a night as this that the missing Ralestone had gone out into the gloom. But he was coming back again, Val reminded himself hurriedly. Of course he was. With a shake he pulled on his trench-coat and slipped out the front door unseen.

14

PIRATE WAYS
ARE HIDDEN WAYS

The rain, fine and needlelike, stung Val's face. There was ominous pools of water gathering in the garden depressions. Even the small stream which bisected their land had grown from a shallow trickle into a thick, mud-streaked roll crowned with foam.

But the bayou was the worst. It had put off its everyday sleepiness with a roar. A chicken coop wallowed by as the boy struggled with the knot of the painter which held the outboard. And after the coop traveled a dead tree, its topmost branches bringing up against the plantation landing with a crack. Val waited for it to whirl on before he got on board his craft.

The adventure was more serious than he had thought. It might not be a case of merely going downstream and into the swamp to the cabin; it might be a case of fighting the rising water in grim battle. Why he did not turn back to the house then and there he never knew. What would have happened if he had? he sometimes speculated afterward. If Ricky had not come into the garden to hunt him? If together they had not—

While Val went with the current, his voyage was ease itself. But when he strove to cut across and so reach the mouth of the hidden swampstream, he narrowly escaped upsetting. As it was, he fended off some dark blot bobbing through he water, his palm meeting it with a force that jarred his bones.

But he did make the mouth of the swampstream. Switching on the strong search-light in the bow, he headed on. And because he was moving now against the current, it seemed that he lost two feet for every one that he advanced.

The muddy water was whipped into foam where it tore around shrub and willow. There were no longer any confining banks, only a waste of water glittering through the dark foliage. The drear habitat of the vultures was being swept bare by the scouring of the incoming streams, but its moldy stench still arose stronger than ever, as if some foulness were being stirred up from its ancient bed.

It was only by chance that Val found the drying rack which marked the boundary of Jeems' property. Here the land was higher than the flood, which had not yet spread inland. He tied the boat to a willow and splashed ashore. In the lower portions of the path his feet sank into patches of wet. Something which might have been—and probably was—a snake oozed away from the beam of his pocket torch.

The clearing was much as it had been, save that the door of the chicken-run stood ajar and its feathered population was gone. But under the cabin Val saw the betraying sparkle of water. The bayou in the rear must have topped flood level.

Someone had been there before him. The lock was battered and there had been an attempt to pry loose its staples, an attempt which had left betraying gouges on the door frame. But misused as it had been, the lock yielded to the key and Val went in. Warned by a lapping sound from beneath it did not take him long to get the chest, relock the door, and head back to the boat.

He was none too soon. Already, in the few moments of his absence, there were rills cutting across the mud, rills which were growing in strength and size. And the flood around the drying rack was up a good three inches. Val dumped the chest into the bow with little ceremony and climbed in after it, his wet trousers clinging damply to his legs. Something plate-armored and possessing wicked yellow eyes swam effortlessly through the light beam—a 'gator bound for the Gulf, whether he would or no.

The return as far as the bayou was easy enough, for again the boat was borne on the current. But when Val faced the torn waters of the river he experienced a certain tightness of throat and chill of blood. What might have been the roof of a small shed was passing lumpily as he hesitated. Then came a tree burdened with a small 'coon which stared at the boy piteously, its eyes green in the light. An eddy sent its ship close to the boat; the top branches clung a moment to the bow. And to Val's surprise, the 'coon roused itself to a mighty effort and crossed into the egg-shell safety the boat offered. Once in the outboard, it retreated to the bow where it crouched beside the chest and kept a wary eye on Val's every movement.

But he could not rescue the wildcat which swept by spitting at the water from a log, nor the shivering doe which awaited the coming of death, marooned on an islet which was fast being cut away by the hungry waters. And all the time the stinging rain fed the flood.

Val gripped the rudder until the bar was printed deep across his palm. Soon it would be too late. He must cross now, heading diagonally downstream to escape the full fury of the current. With a deep breath he turned out into the bayou.

It was like fighting some vast animated featherbed. His greatest efforts were as nothing against the overpowering sweep seaward. And there was constant danger from the floating booty of the storm. The muddy spray lashed his body, filling the bottom of his craft as if it were a tea-cup. And once the boat was whirled almost around.

Val was beginning to wonder just how long a swimmer might last in that black fog of rain, wind, and water when his bow eased into comparatively quiet water. He had crossed the main current; now was the time to head upstream. Grimly he did, to begin a struggle which was to take on all the more horrible properties of a nightmare. For this was many times worse than his fight against the swampstream.

Twice the engine sputtered protestingly and Val thought of trying to leap ashore. But stubbornly the outboard fought on. If there ever were a sturdy ship, fit to be named with Columbus' gallant craft or Hudson's vessel, it was that frail outboard which buffeted the rising waters of a Louisiana bayou gone flood mad.

It achieved the impossible; it crept upstream inch by inch, escaping disaster after disaster by the thinness of a dime. Since he had apparently not been born to drown, Val thought as he saw his headlight touch the tip of the landing, he would doubtless depart this life by hanging.

Then his light picked out something else which lay between him and the landing. The sleek, knife-bowed cruiser certainly did not belong to Pirate's Haven. And what neighbor would come calling by water on such a night? It was moored by two thick ropes to a sunken post, and already the mooring was dragging the bow down. Val headed in toward it, running the outboard between the stranger and the landing.

Out of the blackness ashore a shadow arose and waved at him frenziedly. Then he saw Ricky's white face above her long oil-silk cape. Her hair was plastered tight to her skull and she was protecting her eyes from the fury of the rain with her hands.

Val sent the boat inshore until it bit into the crumbling surface of the levee with a shock which threatened his balance. Ricky snatched at the painter and held steady while he jumped. They made the boat fast and Val landed the chest. The passenger did his own disembarking, making his way into the garden without a backward look. Then Val demanded an explanation.

"What are you doing here?" he tried to outscreech the wind.

In answer she clapped her wet, muddy hand across his mouth and pulled him back from the levee.

They reached the semi-shelter of a rotting summerhouse where he put down the chest. Ricky pushed her wet hair out of her eyes. It was impossible for them to hear each other without screaming madly.

"Jeems told me—after you left—Val! How could you be so mad!"

"I made it." He touched the chest with his toe. "After we had practically kidnapped him, we couldn't let his belongings just float away. But why are you out here? And where did that boat come from?"

"I came out here after Jeems told me. I'm all right." She laughed shakily. "I've got my oldest clothes on—and this," she touched her cape. "I couldn't stay in there—waiting—after I knew. And I didn't want Rupert to ask questions. So I said that I was going to bed with a headache. Then I slipped out here to the levee. And I hadn't been here two minutes before that boat came downstream. There were four men in it and they got out and went into the bushes over there. And, Val, Rupert is down at the other end of the garden where they are having trouble with the levee. Holmes and Creighton went down to see if they could help, too, just after you left. There's nobody but

Charity up at the house with Lucy and Letty-Lou. Val, what are we going to do?'' she appealed to him.

"First I'll investigate these visitors," he said easily, though he felt far from easy within.

"Me too," she said firmly if ungrammatically, and since Val could not wait to argue, she went along.

They took the route she had watched the invaders follow, wriggling through wet bushes and around trees.

"Val, look out!" She grabbed his arm and so saved him from tumbling headlong into a black hole in the ground. Vines and a small shrub or two had been ruthlessly torn out to bare the opening. It was here that the visitors must have gone to earth. And then Val had a glimmering of the truth; the "Boss" and his friends had at last found Jeems' private door.

Prudence urged that they return to the house and send Sam Two or some other messenger down to the cross-roads store to summon the police by phone. Prudence however had never successfully advised any Ralestone. They had a decided taste for fighting their own battles. So, torch in hand, Val dropped into the hole. And a moment later Ricky slid do to join him.

They stood in a rough passage. Stout timbers banked its sides and guarded the roof. There was a damp underground smell such as Val had noted in the cellar of the house, but the air was fresh enough. After the first hasty survey, the boy held his fingers over the bulb of the flash-light so that only the faintest glimmer escaped to light their path.

The passage was short, ending abruptly in a low bricked

room. Save for themselves, a tangle of rotting rope in a far corner, and two lively black beetles, it was empty.

"Val," Ricky's throaty whisper reached him, "can't you guess what this is? The first pirate Ralestone's storage-house!"

It was a likely enough explanation—though nothing could have been stored there very long; the place was too damp. Beads of slimy moisture from the walls dripped slowly down, shining like silver in the light.

At the other side of the room was a corridor branching away. But this they barely glanced into, little knowing how that neglect was to prove disastrous in the end. It was the main door to their right which interested them most, for that led, so far as Val could determine, toward the house. And that must have been the one the mysterious visitors had followed.

Thus they came into the second of their pirate ancestor's store-rooms. This one was long and narrow. Three wooden casks eaten with decay and spotted with fungus stood against the wall, testifying to the use to which this chamber had been put, though the all-pervading damp could not have been good for the wine.

Again a dark archway tempted them on, and the third room into which they came had a more grim reminder of the scarlet past of the house. For Ricky stumbled over something which clinked dully. And when Val used the flash they looked down upon a telltale length of chain ending in an iron ring, its other end soldered into the wall.

"Val," Ricky's voice quavered, "did—did they keep people here?"

"Slaves, perhaps," her brother answered soberly and shoved the rusting metal aside with his foot. But there were two other chains hanging from the wall, speaking of past horrors of which he did not care to think.

And then as their light picked out these damning testimonials, Val thought that the Ralestones, for all their pride and fine, brave airs, had been only pirates after all, akin to those whom they were now hunting through the dark.

There was a low arched doorway of brick on the right side of the room, and this they passed through. Beyond were three broad stone steps, worn a little on the treads, one cracked clear across. These led to a wide landing paved with brick. Here the walls were brick as well. Ricky touched one involuntarily and drew back her hand with a little exclamation of disgust. She wiped her palm vigorously on the wet surface of her cape.

Everywhere was the smell of rot and slow, vile decay. In spite of its historical associations, decided Val, this vault should be sealed forever from the daylight and left to the sole occupancy of those nameless things which creep in its dark. The very air, in spite of its freshness, seemed tainted.

Another flight of stairs was before them, the treads fashioned of stone but equipped with a rotted wooden hand-rail. And above was the faint reflection of light and the sound of voices. Val hesitated and realized for the first time how foolhardy their expedition was.

Those above would be prepared to handle interruptions. Val was determined to keep Ricky out of trouble, and to go on alone was the rankest folly. But, as he hesitated, the decision was taken out of his hands, for the light above suddenly became brighter. Grabbing at Ricky's arm, he stumbled back into the shelter of the archway, pulling her after him.

A round circle of light shone plainly at the top of the stairs. Someone was coming down. Ricky's breath was warm on Val's cheek and she moved with a faint crackling of her cape which sounded as loud as a thunderclap in his ears.

"How're we gonna do it without bustin' the wall down?" demanded an aggrieved voice from the top of the stairs. "There ain't no knob, no handle, no nothin' to work it from this side. And these guys what stored their stuff here in the boot-leggin' days never got into the house."

"The boy got through, didn't he?" Val knew that voice, the Boss of the swamp meeting. "Well, if he did, we can."

"Lissen, Boss, it's a secret, ain't it? An' we gotta know how it works before we can work it. An' lissen here, you swamp bum, you keep outta my way—see? I don't care if you were one of Mike Flannigan's boys; that don't cut no ice with me." This truculent warning must have been addressed to an unseen companion on the same stair level. The listeners below heard a faint sound which might have marked a collision and then the hiss of swamp French spoken hurriedly and angrily.

"What're you gonna do now, Boss?"

The light half-way down the stairs paused. "There is some way of opening that panel—"

"An' we gotta find it. All right, all right. But tell me how."

"I don't know whether it will be necessary to open it—from this side."

"What d'ya mean?"

"Use that thick skull of yours, Red. Doors swing two ways, don't they? They can be used either to go in or to go out."

"Got it!" The thick voice was oily with flattering approval. "We can get out this way—"

"Smart work, Red. Did you think that out all by yourself?" asked the other contemptuously. "Yes, we can come out this way when"—his voice was sharp with purpose—"we are finished. Send one of these swampers down to the levee where the men are working. As long as this flood keeps rising we're safe. Then the other three of us will go for the house. We may be seen that way, but there's no use spending any more time here playing tick-tack-toe on that wood up there. We locate what we want, and if we're cornered we can come out through here to the bayou. Slick enough."

"Great stuff, Boss—" Red began. But the rest was muffled, for Ricky and Val drew back into the room of the chains. There was only one thing to do now—reach Rupert and the others and prepare to meet these skulkers in the open. But before they had quite crossed the room Ricky came to grief. She caught her foot in one of those gruesome chains and stumbled forward, falling on her hands and knee. The noise of her fall echoed around the low chamber with betraying clamor.

A white light beat upon them as Val stooped to aid Ricky.

"Stop!" came the shout, but Val had only one thought, to dim that light. He swung back his arm and flung his own flash straight at the other. There was a grunt of pain and the light fell to the floor. With the tinkle of breaking glass it went out. Val pulled Ricky to her feet and threw her toward the door, forgetting everything but the wild panic which urged him out of that place of foul darkness. They bruised their hands against the brick as they felt for the opening, and then they were out in the other chamber.

"Val," Ricky clung to him, "I've got that little flash I keep under my pillow at night. Wait a minute until I get it out of my pocket. We can't find our way out of here without a light."

Muffled sounds from behind them suggested that their pursuers were on the trail even without light. After all, given time enough, it would be easy for them to feel their way out of the vaults. Val hustled Ricky on, taking his direction from one of the wine-casks he had bumped into. And before he allowed her to hunt for her torch they stood in the first of the chambers.

The light she produced was poor and it flickered warningly. But it was good enough for them to see the dark opening which led to the outer world. They ducked into this just as the first of the other party came cursing into the open. At Val's orders, Ricky switched off the light and they crept along by the wall, one hand on its guiding surface.

But the way seemed longer than it had upon their entering. Surely they should have reached the garden entrance by now. And the surface underfoot remained level instead of slanting upward. Suddenly Ricky gave a little cry.

"We've taken the wrong passage! There's only a blank wall in front of us!"

She was right. The torch showed a brick surface across their path, and Val remembered too late the second passage out of the first chamber. They must go back and hope to elude the others in the dark.

"They may have all gone out, thinking we were still ahead of them," he mused aloud.

"Well, it's got to be done," Ricky observed, "so we might as well do it."

Back they went along the unknown passage. This appeared to run straight out from the first chamber. But why it had been fashioned and then walled up they had no way of knowing. Ricky's torch picked out the entrance at last.

"Wait," Val cautioned her, "we had better see how the land lies before we go out in the open."

They stood listening. Save for the constant drip, drip of water, there was no sound.

"I guess it's clear," he said.

"Wonder where all the water is coming from?" Ricky shivered.

"Down from the garden. Come on, I think it's safe to have a light now."

Ricky must have been holding the torch upward when she pressed the button, for the round circle of light appeared on the supporting timbers above the door. They both looked up, fascinated for a moment. The old oak had been laid in a crisscross pattern, the best support possible in the days when the vaults had been made.

"How wet—" began Ricky.

Val cried out suddenly and struck at her. The blow sent her sprawling some three or four feet back in the passage. There might be time yet to cover her body with his own, he planned desperately, before—

The sound of slipping earth was all about them as Val flung himself toward Ricky. As he thrust blindly at her body, rolling her back farther into the tunnel, he felt the first clod strike full upon his shoulder. Ricky's complaining whimper was the last thing he heard clearly. For out of the dark came the crash of breaking timber.

He was felled by a stroke across the upper arm, and then followed a chill darkness in which he was utterly swallowed up.

15

PIECES OF EIGHT—
RALESTONES' FATE!

Through the dull roaring which filled his ears Val heard a
sharp call:

"Val! Val, where are you? Val!"

He stared up into utter blackness.

"Val!"

"Here, Ricky!" But that thin thread of a whisper surely
didn't belong to him. He tried again and achieved a sort of
croak. Something moved behind him and there was an
answering rattle of falling clods.

"Val, I'm afraid to move," her voice wavered unsteadily.
"It seems to be falling yet. Where are you?"

The boy tried to investigate, only to find himself more securely fastened than if he had been scientifically bound. And now that the mists had cleared from him, his spine and back felt a sharp pain to which he was no stranger. From his breast-bone down he was held as if in a vise.

"Are you hurt, Ricky?" He formed the words slowly. Every breath he drew thrust a red-hot knife between his ribs. He turned his head toward her, pillowing his cheek on the gritty clay.

"No. But where are you, Val? Can't you come to me?"

"Sorry. Un—unavoidably detained," he gasped. "Don't try any crawling or the rest may come down on us."

"Val! What's the matter? Are you hurt?" Her questions cut sharply through the darkness.

"Banged up a little. No"—he heard the rustle which betrayed her movements—"don't try to come to me—Please, Ricky!"

But with infinite caution she came, until her brother felt the edge of her cape against his face. Then her questing hand touched his throat and slid downward to his shoulders.

"Val!" He knew what horror colored that cry as she came upon what imprisoned him.

"It's all right, Ricky. I'm just pinned in. If I don't try to move I'm safe." Quickly he tried to reassure her.

"Val, don't lie to me now—you're hurt!"

"It's not bad, really, Ricky—"

"Oh!" There was a single small cry and a moment of utter silence and then a hurried rustling.

"Here." Her hand groped for his head. "I've wadded up my cape. Can I slip it under your head?"

"Better not try just yet. Anything might send off the landslide again. Just—just give me a minute or two to—to sort of catch my breath." Catch his breath, when every sobbing gasp he drew was a stab!

"Can't we—can't I lift some of the stuff off?" she asked.

"No. Too risky."

"But—but we can't stay here—,' Her voice trailed off and it was then that she must have realized for the first time just what had happened to them.

"I'm afraid we'll have to, Ricky," said her brother quietly.

"But, Val—Val, what if—if—"

"If we aren't found?" he put her fear into words. "But we will be. Rupert is doubtless moving a large amount of earth right now to accomplish that."

"Rupert doesn't know where we are." She had regained control of both voice and spirit. "We—we may never be found, Val."

"I was a fool," he stated plainly a fact which he now knew to be only too true.

"I would have come even if you hadn't, Val," she answered generously and untruthfully. It was perhaps the kindest thing she had ever said.

Now that the noise of the catastrophe had died away they could hear again the drip of water. And that sound tortured Val's dry throat. A glass of cool water—He turned his head restlessly.

"If we only had a light," came Ricky's wish.

"The flash is probably buried."

203

"Val, will—will it be fun?"

"What?" he demanded, suddenly alert at her tone. Had the dark and their trouble made her light-headed?

"Being a ghost. We—we could walk the hall with Great-uncle Rick; he wouldn't begrudge us that."

"Ricky! Stop it!"

Her answering laugh, though shaky, was sane enough.

"I do pick the wrong times to display my sense of humor, don't I? Val, is it so very bad?"

Something within him crumbled at that question.

"Not so good, Lady," he replied in spite of the resolutions he had made.

She brushed back the hair glued by perspiration to his forehead. Ricky was not gold, he thought, for gold is a rather dirty thing. But she was all steel, as clean and shining as a blade fresh from the hands of a master armorer. He made a great effort and found that he could move his right arm an inch or two. Concentrating all his strength there, he wriggled it back and forth until he could draw it free from the wreckage. But his left shoulder and side were numb save for the pain which came and went.

"Got my arm free," Val told her exultantly and reached up to feel for her in the dark. His fingers closed upon coarse cloth. He pulled feebly and something rolled toward him.

"What's this?"

Ricky's hands slid along his arm to the thing he had found. He could hear her exploring movements.

"It's some sort of a bundle. I wonder where it came from."

"Some more remains of the jolly pirate days, I suppose."

"Here's something else. A bag, I think. Ugh! It smells nasty! There's a hole in it— Oh, here's a piece of money. At least it feels like money. There's more in the bag." She pressed a disk about as large as a half-dollar into Val's palm.

"Pirate loot—" he began. Anything that would keep them from thinking of where they were and what had happened was to be welcomed.

"Val"—he could hear her move uneasily—"remember that old saying: "Pieces of eight—Ralestones' fate?"

"All good families have curses," he reminded her.

"And good families can have—can have accidents, too."

There could be no answer to that. Nor did Val feel like answering. The savage pain in his legs and back had given way to a kind of numbness. A chill not caused by the dank air crawled up his body. What—what if his injuries were worse than he had thought? What if—if—

The dripping of the water seemed louder, and it no longer fell with the same rhythm. Ricky must be counting money from the bag. He could hear the clink of metal against stone as she dropped a piece.

"Don't lose it," he muttered foggily.

"Lose what?"

"Your pieces of eight."

"What do you mean?"

"I haven't touched— Val, do—do you feel worse?"

But he had no thought now for his body. If Ricky had not dropped the money, then what had caused the clink? He ground his cheek against the clay. *Thud, thud, clink, thud*. That was not water dripping nor coin rattling. That was the sound of digging. And digging meant—

"Ricky! They're digging! I can hear them!"

Her fingers closed about his free hand until the nails dug into the flesh. "Where?"

"I don't know. Listen!"

The sound had grown in strength until now, though muffled, it sounded through that part of the passage still remaining open.

"It comes from this end. From behind that wall. But why should it come from there?"

"Does it matter? Val, do you suppose they could hear me if I pounded on the wall at this side?"

"You haven't anything heavy enough to pound with."

"Yes, I have. This package thing that you found. It's quite heavy. Val, we've got to let them know we're here!"

She crawled away, moving with caution lest she bring on another slide. That reassuring *thud, thud* still sounded. Then, after long minutes, Val heard the answering blow from their side. Three times Ricky struck before the rhythm of the digging was broken. Then there was silence followed by three sharp blows. They had heard!

Ricky beat a perfect tattoo in joy and was quickly answered. Then the *thud, thud* began again, but this time the pace was quickened.

"They've heard! They're coming!" Ricky's voice shrilled until it became a scream. "Val, we're found!"

A clod was loosened somewhere above them and crashed upon the wreckage. Would the efforts of their rescuers bring on another slide?

"Be quiet, Ricky," Val croaked a warning. "it's still moving."

Then there came the sharp clink of metal against stone. "Val," called Ricky, "they're right against the wall now!"

"Come back here, away from it. We—we don't want you caught, too," he answered her.

Obediently she crawled back to him and again he felt her hand close about his. The sound of metal grating against stubborn brick filled their pocket of safety. But as an ominous accompaniment came the soft hiss of earth sliding onto the wreckage. Which would win to them first, the rescuers or the second slide?

There was a vicious grinding noise from the walled end of the passage. A moment later a blinding ray of light swung in, to focus upon them.

"Ricky! Val!"

Val was blinking stupidly at the light, but Ricky had presence of mind enough to answer.

"Here we are!"

"Look out," Val roused enough to warn, "the walls are unsafe!"

"We're coming through," rang the answer out of the dark. "Stand away!"

Now that they could see, Val realized for the first time the danger of their position. A jagged, water-rotten beam half covered with clay and sand lay across him, and beyond that was a mass of splintered wood and wet earth. A little sick, he looked up at Ricky. She was staring at the wreckage. Her eyes were black in a white, mud-smeared face.

"Val—Val!" His name came as the thinnest of whispers.

"It isn't as bad as it looks," he said hurriedly. "Something underneath must be supporting most of the weight or—or I wouldn't be here at all."

"Val," she repeated, and then, paying no heed to his frantic injunctions to keep away, she dug at earth and rotten wood with her hands. Using the long bundle clumsily wrapped in stained canvas, she levered a piece of beam out of the way so that she might get down on her knees and scoop up the sand and clay.

"Ricky! Val!" The light swung ahead as someone scrambled through the hole in the barrier wall. Then, when the ray held firm upon them, the headlong rush was checked for a long instant. "Val!"

"Get her—away," he begged. "Another—slip—"

But before he had done, a long arm gathered Ricky up as if she had been a child. "Right," came the firm answer. "Sam, take Miss 'Chanda back. Then—"

Val was watching the reflection of the flash on the broken roof above him. Sand slid in tiny streams down the wall, mingling with the greenish trickles of water. There were queer blue and green arcs painted on the brick which had something to do with the hot pain behnid his eyes. The blue turned to orange—to scarlet—

"Careful! Right here in the hall, Holmes—"

The broken earth above him had somehow been changed to a high celing, the chill darkness to blazing light and warmth.

"Ricky?" he asked.

"Here, Val." Her face was very close to his.

"You—are—all—right?"

208

" 'Course!" But she was crying. "Don't try to talk, Val. You must be quiet."

He heard someone moving toward them but he kept his eyes on Ricky's face. "We did it!"

"Yes," she answered slowly, "we did it."

"Val, don't try to talk." Rupert's face showed above Ricky's hunched shoulder. There was an odd, strained look about his mouth, a smear of mud across his cheek. But the harsh tone of his voice struck his brother as dumb as if he had slapped him.

"Sorry," Val shaped the words stiffly, "all my fault."

"Nothing's your fault," Ricky's indignant answer cut in. "But—but just be quiet, Val, until the doctor comes."

He turned his head slowly. On the hearth-stone stood Charity talking quietly to Holmes. Just within the circle of the firelight lay a bundle which he had seen before. But of course, that was the thing they had found in the passage, which Ricky had used to pound out their answer to Rupert.

"Ricky—" Val always believed that it was some instinct out of the past which forced that whisper out of him—"Ricky, open that package."

"Why—" she began, but then she got to her feet and went to the bundle, twisting the tarred rope that fastened it in a vain attempt to undo the intricate knots. It was Holmes who produced a knife and sawed through the tough cord. And it was Holmes who unrolled the strips of canvas, oil-silk, and greasy skins. But it was Ricky who took up what lay within and held it out so that it reflected both red firelight and golden room light.

Her brother's sigh was one of satisfaction.

For Ricky held aloft by its ponderous hilt a great war sword. There could be no doubt in any of them—the Luck of Lorne had returned.

"We found it!" breathed Ricky.

"Put it in its place," Val ordered.

Without a word, Rupert drew out a chair and scrambled up. Taking from Ricky's hands the ancient weapon, he slipped it into the niche their pirate ancestor had made for it. In spite of the years underground, the metal of hilt and blade was clear. Seven hundred years of history—their Luck!

"Everything will come right again,', Val repeated as Ricky came back to him. "You'll see. Everything—will—be—all—right."

His eyes closed in spite of his efforts. He was back in the darkness where he could only feel the warmth of Ricky's hands clasped about his.

16

RALESTONES STAND TOGETHER

"I like Louisiana," drawled Holmes lazily from his perch on the window-seat. "The most improbable things happen here. One finds secret passages under houses and medieval war swords stuck in drains. Then there are 'things that go boomp in the night,' too. It might be worth settling down here—"

"Not for you," cut in Charity briskly. "Too far from the bright lights for you, my man."

"Just for that," he triumphed, "I shall not return this lost property found under a cushion of the couch in the hall."

At the sight of that familiar black note-book, Val shifted uneasily on his pillows. Rupert got up.

"Tired, old man?" he asked and reached to straighten one of his brother's feather-stuffed supports.

Val shook his head. Being bandaged like a mummy was wearying, but one had to humor two broken ribs and a fractured collar-bone.

"Sometimes," replied Charity, "you are just too clever, Mr. Judson Holmes. That does not happen to be my property."

"No?" He flipped it open and held it up so that she might see what lay within. "I'll admit that it isn't your usual sort of stuff, but—"

She was staring at the drawings. "No, that isn't mine. But who—"

Ricky got up from the end of Val's cot and went to look. Then she turned, her eyes shining with excitement. "You're trying them again! But, Val, you said you never would."

"Give me that book!" he ordered grimly. But Rupert had calmly collected the trophy and was turning over the pages one by one. Val made a horrible face at Ricky and resigned himself to the inevitable.

"How long have you been doing this sort of thing?" his brother asked as he turned the last page.

"Ever so long," Ricky answered for Val brightly. "He used to draw whole letters from them when we were at school. There were two sets, one for good days and the other for bad."

"And now," Val cut in, "suppose we just forget the whole matter. Will you please let me have that!"

"Rupert, don't let him go all modest on us now," urged the demon sister. "One retiring violet in the family is enough."

"And who is the violet? Your charming self?" inquired Holmes.

"No." Ricky smiled pleasantly. "Only Mr. Creighton might be interested in the contents of Bluebeard's Chamber. What do you think, Rupert?"

At that audacious hint, Val remembered the night of the storm and Ricky's strange attitude then.

"So Rupert's the missing author," he commented lightly. "Well, well, well."

Charity's indulgent smile faded, and Holmes, suddenly alert, leaned forward. Rupert stared at Val for a long moment, his face blank. Was he going to retire behind his wall of reserve from which their venture underground had routed him? Or was he going to remain the very human person who had spent eight hours of every day at his brother's beck and call for the past few weeks?

"Regular Charlie Chan, aren't you?" he asked mildly.

Val's sigh of relief was echoed by Ricky. "Thanks—so much," Val replied humbly in the well-known manner of the famous detective Rupert had likened him to.

"Then we are right?" asked Ricky.

Rupert's eyebrows slid upward. "You seemed too sure to be in doubt," he commented.

"Well, I was sure at times. But then no one can ever be really sure of anything about you," she admitted frankly.

"But why—" protested Charity.

"Why didn't I spread the glad tidings that I was turning out the great American novel?" he asked. "I don't know. Perhaps I am a violet—no?" He looked pained at Ricky's snort of dissent. "Or perhaps I just don't like to talk about things which may never come true. When I didn't hear from Lever, I thought that my worst forebodings were realized and that my scribbling was worthless. But you know," he paused to fill his pipe, "writing is more or less like the drug habit. I've told stories all my life, and I found myself tied to my typewriter in spite of my disappointment. As for talking about it—well, how much has Val ever said about these?" He ruffled the pages of the note-book provokingly.

"Nothing. And you would never have seen those if I could have prevented it," his brother replied. "Those are for my private satisfaction only."

"Two geniuses in one family." Ricky rolled her eyes heavenward. "This is almost too, too much!"

"Jeems," Val ordered, "you're the nearest. Can't you make her shut up?"

"Just let him try," said his sister sweetly. The swamper grinned but made no move to stir from his chair.

Jeems had become as much a part of Pirate's Haven as the Luck, which Val could see from his cot glimmering dully in its niche in the Long Hall. The swamper's confinement in the sick-room had paled his heavy tan and he had lost the sullen frown which had made him appear so old and bitter. Now, dressed in a pair of Val's white slacks and a shirt from his wardrobe, Jeems was as much at ease in his surroundings as Rupert or Holmes.

It had been Jeems who had saved Ricky and Val on that night of terror when they had been trapped in the secret ways of their private ancestors. Sam Two had trailed Ricky to the garden and had witnessed their entering the tunnel. But fear of the dark unknown had kept him from venturing in after them. So he had lingered there long enough to see the invaders come out and take to the river. Catching some words of theirs about a cave-in, he had gone pelting off to Rupert with the story.

The investigating party from the levee had discovered, to their horror, the passage choked for half its length. They were making a futile and dangerous attempt to clear it when Jeems appeared on the scene. Letty-Lou having given him a garbled account of events, he had staggered from his bed in an effort to reach Rupert. He alone knew the underground ways as well as he knew the garden. And so once getting Rupert's attention, he had set them to work in the cellar cutting through to the one passage which paralleled the foundation walls.

In the weeks which followed their emergence from the threatened tomb, the swamper had unobtrusively slipped into a place in the household. While Val was frightening his family by indulging in a bout of fever to complicate his injuries, Jeems was proving himself a tower of strength and a person to be relied upon. Even Lucy had once asked his opinion on the importance of a fire in the hall, and with that his position was assured.

Of the invaders they had heard or seen no more, although the police had visited Pirate's Haven on two separate occasions, interviewing each and every member of the household. They had also made a half-hearted attempt to search the swamp. But for all the evidence they found, Ricky and Val might have been merely indulging in an over-vivid dream. Save that the Luck hung again in the Long Hall.

"Seriously, though," Holmes drew Val's thoughts out of the past, "these are worth-while. Would you mind if I showed them to a friend of mine who might be interested?"

Since Rupert had already nodded and Charity had handed him the note-book, Val decided that he could hardly raise a protest.

"Rupert," Charity glanced at him, "are you going to see Creighton?"

"Since all has been discovered," he misquoted, "I suppose that that is all there is left for me to do."

"Then you had better do it today; he's planning to leave for the North tonight," she informed him.

Rupert came to life. For all his pose of unconcern, he was excited. In the long days Val had been tied to the cot hurriedly set up in a corner of the drawing-room on the night of the rescue—it had been thought wiser to move him no farther than necessary—he had found again the real Rupert they had known of old. There was little he could conceal from his younger brother now—or so Val thought.

"Sam has the convertible," Rupert said. "There's something wrong with the brakes and I told him to take it to town and have it looked over. Goodness only knows what time he'll be back."

"See here, Ralestone," Holmes looked at his wrist-watch, "I've the car I rented here with me. Let me drive you in. Charity has to go, anyway, and see about sending off those sketches of hers."

"Oh, but we were going together," protested Ricky. "I have some shopping to do."

"Very simple," Val suggested. "Why don't you all go?"

"But that would leave you alone." Rupert shook his head.

"No. There's Jeems."

"I don't know," Rupert hesitated doubtfully.

"It doesn't reqire more than one person to wait on me at present," Val said firmly. "Now all of you go. But remember, I shall expect the Greeks to return bearing gifts."

Holmes saluted. "Right you are, my hearty. Well, ladies, the chariot awaits without."

In spite of their protests, Val at last got rid of them. Since he had a project of his own, he was only too glad to see the last of his oversolicitous family for awhile.

Val had never been able to understand why broken ribs or a fractured collar-bone should chain one to the bed. And since he had recovered from his wrenched back he was eager to be up and around. In private, with the protesting assistance of Sam Two, he had made a pilgrimage across the room and back. And now it was his full intention to be seated on the terrace when the family came home.

It was Lucy of all people who aided fortune to give him his opportunity.

"Mistuh Val," she announced from the doorway as the sound of the car pulling out of the drive signaled the departure of the city-bound party, "them light's out agin."

"Another fuse gone? That's the second this week. Who's been playing games?" he asked.

"This no-'count!" She dragged out of hiding from behind her voluminous skirts her second son, a infant who rejoiced in the name of Gustavus Adolphus and was generally called "Doff." At that moment he was sobbing noisily and eyeing Val as if the boy were the Grand High Executioner of Tartary. "Yo' tell Mistuh Val what yos doin'!" commanded his mother, emphasizing her order with a shake.

"Ain't done nothin'," wailed Doff. "Sam give me a nickle an' say, 'Le's hab fun.' I puts the nickle in lil' hole, then Mammy catched me."

"Doff seems to be the victim, Lucy," Val observed. "Where's Sam?"

"Don' know. But I'm a-goin' to fin' out!" she stated with ominous determination. "How I'm a-goin' git ironin' done when dere ain't no heat fo' de iron, I asks yo'?"

"There are some fuses in the pantry and Jeems will put one in for you," Val promised.

With a sniff Lucy withdrew, her fingers still hooked in the collar of her tearful son. Jeems glanced at Val as he went by the boy's cot. And Val didn't care for what he read into that glance. Had the swamper by any foul chance come to suspect Val's little plan?

218

But it all turned out just as he had hoped. Val made that most momentous trip in four easy stages, resting on the big chair where Rupert had spent so many hours, on the bench by the window, in the first of the deck-chairs by the side of the French doors leading to the terrace, and then he reached the haven of the last deck-chair and settled down just where he had intended. And when Jeems returned there was nothing he could do but accept the fact that Val had fled the cot.

"Miss Ricky won't like this," he prophesied darkly. "Nor Mr. Rupert neither. Yo' wouldn't've tried if they'd been heah."

"Oh, stop worrying. If you'd been tied to that cot the way I've been, you'd be glad to get out here, too. It's great!"

The sun was warm but the afternoon shadow of an oak overhung his seat so that Val escaped the direct force of the rays. A few feet away Satan sprawled full length, giving a fine imitation of a cat that had rid himself of all nine lives, or at least of eight and a half.

Never had the garden shown so rich a green. Ricky's care had sharpened the lines of the flower-beds and had set shrubs in their proper places. And the plants had repaid her with a riot of blossoms. A breeze set the gray moss to swaying from the branches of the oak. And a green grass-hopper crossed the terrace in four great leaps, almost scraping Satan's ear in a fashion which might easily have been fatal to the insect. Val sighed and slipped down lower in his chair. "It's great," he murmured again.

"Sure is," Jeems echoed. He dropped down cross-legged beside Val, disdaining the other chair.

Satan stretched without opening his eyes and yawned, gaping to the fullest extent of his jaws, his tongue rising so that it seemed pointed like a snake's. Then he rolled over on his other side and curled up with his paws under his chin. A bumblebee blundered by Val's head on its way to visit the morning-glories. He suddenly discovered it difficult to keep his eyes open.

"Someone's comin'," observed Jeems. "Ah just heard a car turn in from the road."

"But the folks have been gone such a short time," Val protested.

However, the car which came almost noiselessly down the drive was not the one in which the family had departed. It had the shape of a sleek gray beetle, rounded so that it was difficult to tell at first glance the hood from the rear. It glided to a stop before the steps and after a moment four passengers disembarked.

Val simply stared, but Jeems got to his feet in one swift movement.

For, coming purposefully up the terrace steps, were four men they had seen before and had very good cause to remember for the rest of their lives.

In the lead strutted the rival, a tight smile rendering his unlovely features yet more disagreeable. Behind him trotted the red-faced counselor who had accompanied him on his first visit. But matching the rival step for step was the "Boss," while "Red" brought up the rear in a tidy fashion.

"Swell place, ain't it?" demanded the rival, taking no notice of Val or Jeems. "Make yourselves to home, boys; the place is yours."

Val gripped the arm of his chair. Sam, Rupert, Holmes— they were all beyond call. It was left to him to meet this unbelievable invasion alone. There was a stir beside him. Val glanced up to meet the slightest of reassuring nods from the swamper. Jeems was with him.

"Whatcha gonna do with the joint, Brick?" asked Red, tossing his cigarette down on the flagstones and grinding it to powder with his heel.

"I dunno yet." The rival strode importantly toward the front door.

"You might tell us when you find out," Val suggested quietly.

With an exaggerated start of surprise the rival turned toward the boy.

"Oh, so it's you, kid?"

"Perhaps," Val said softly, "you had better introduce your friends. After all, I like to know the names of my guests."

The Boss smiled sardonically and Red grinned. Only the red-faced lawyer shuffled his feet uneasily and looked from one to another of his companions with an expression of pleading. But the rival came directly to the point.

"Where's that high and mighty brother of yours?" he demanded.

"Mr. Ralestone will doubtless be very glad to see you," Val evaded, having no desire for the visitors to discover just how slender his resources were. "Jeems, you might go and tell him that we have visitors. Go through the Long Hall, it's nearer that way." He dug the fingernails of his sound hand into the soft wood of the chair arm. Could Jeems interpret that hint? Someone must remove and hide the Luck before these men saw it.

"Right." The swamper turned on his heel and padded toward the French windows.

"No, you don't!" the rival snarled as he moved into line between Jeems and his objective. "When we want that guy, we'll hunt him out ourselves. When we're good and ready!"

"If you don't wish to see my brother, just why did you come?" Val asked feverishly. He must keep them talking there until he had time to think of some way of getting that slender blade of steel into hiding.

"We're movin' in," Red answered casually for them all.

"How interesting. I think that the police will enjoy hearing that," Val commented.

"It's perfectly legal," bleated the lawyer. "We possess a court order to view the place with the purpose of appraising it for sale." He drew a stiff paper from the inside pocket of his coat and waved it toward the boy.

"Bunk! I don't know much about the law but I do know that you could have obtained nothing of the kind without our being notified. And just which one of you has been selected to do the appraising?"

"Him," answered Red laconically and jerked his thumb at the Boss.

"So," Jeems stared at him, "since yo' couldn't git what yo' want by thievin' at night, yo're goin' to try and git it by day."

"But what are you really after? I'm curious to know. You certainly don't want a sugar plantation which hasn't been paying its way since the Civil War. That just isn't reasonable. And you ought to know that we can't afford to buy you off. We must be living over a gold-mine that we haven't discovered. Come on, tell us where it is," Val prodded.

"Cut the cackle," advised Red, "an' let's git down to it."

"I would advise you to get back in your car and drive out." Val wondered if his face looked as stiff as it felt. "This visit isn't going to get you anywhere."

"We ain't goin' any place, kid," remarked the rival. "You don't seem to understand. We're stayin' right here. I got rights and the judge has recognized them. I'm top guy here now."

"Yeah. Yuh ain't so smart as yuh think yuh are," contributed Red, scowling at Val. "We ain't gonna leave."

It wasn't Red's speech, however, that straightened the boy's back and made Jeems shift his position an inch or two. There was another car coming up the drive. And since their enemies were all gathered before them, they could only be receiving friends, or at the worst neutrals.

But the car which came from between the liveoaks to park behind the first contained only two passengers. LeFleur and Creighton got out, stopped in surprise to view the party on the terrace, and then came up, shoving by Red.

"Quite a party," Val observed. "But how did you manage to arrive so opportunely?"

"We have made a discovery," panted the Creole lawyer; "a very important discovery. What are these men doing here?"

"We got a court order to view this house for sale." The rival was truculent. "An' it's all legal. The mouthpiece says so," he indicated his counselor.

"Perhaps," Creighton's cool tones cut through, "you had better introduce us." There was a decided change in his manner. Gone was his shy nervousness, his slightly hesitant reserve. It was a keen business man who stood there now.

Val grinned. "You see before you the family skeleton. May I introduce Mr. Ralestone, who firmly believes that he is the Ralestone of Pirate's Haven? And three other—shall we say gentlemen—whom I myself have never met formally. Though I did have the pleasure, I believe," he addressed the Boss directly, "of blackening your eye."

"Yeah, I'm Ralestone, and I'm gonna have my rights," stated the rival briskly.

"You are a descendant of Roderick Ralestone?" asked Leleur.

"Yuh know I am. I got proofs!"

"The man is a liar," Creighton said calmly.

As they stared at him, LeFleur nodded. Val saw an ugly grin begin to curve Red's thick lips.

"Yeah? An how do yuh know that, wise guy?" he asked.

"Because there is only one Roderick Ralestone in this generation and he is standing right there. Permit me to introduce Roderick St. Jean Ralestone!"

The person he turned to was Jeems!

17

THE RETURN OF RICK RALESTONE

Val ventured to break the sudden silence which resulted from Creighton's astonishing statement.

"But how—why—"

"Yeah," the rival had collected a measure of his scattered wits, "whatta yuh mean, wise guy?"

"Just this—" LeFleur drew himself up and faced the invaders sternly—"I have only this very morning deposited with the probate court certain documents making very plain the identity of this young man. Without the shadow of a doubt he is the only living descendant of Roderick Ralestone and his wife, Valerie St. Jean de Roche. I have also sworn out a complaint—"

226

Then the Boss took a hand in the game. "The boy's a minor," he observed.

"Through me," LeFleur returned, "Mr. Rupert Ralestone as nearest of kin has applied for guardianship and there will be no difficulty in the settlement of that matter."

"Yeah!" The rival threw his gloves on the terrace and glared not at LeFleur but at his own backing. Having stared at the lawyer of his party until that unfortunate man lost all assurance, he attacked the Boss. "So, wise guy, what now? We ain't got such a snap as yuh said we were gonna have. We were gonna move right in and take over the joint, were we? We didn't have anything to worry about. For once we was playin' with the law. Yeah, we were. We are nothin' but a gang of mugs. Whatta we gonna do now, huh? You oughta know. Ain't yuh been doin' our thinkin' for us all along? We can't grab the land and run. We gotta camp right here if we're gonna git anything. And how are we gonna—"

"Simpson!" the Boss's voice was sharp. "Be quiet! You are becoming wearisome. Gentlemen," he bowed slightly toward LeFleur and Creighton, "one cannot fight bad luck, and this time Fate smiles upon you. It was a good idea if it had worked," he added musingly. "Young Ralestone seems to have gathered all the aces into his hand. Even," the drawl became a sneer, "even the guardianship of the missing heir, which will mean a nice sum in the bank for the happy guardian, if all reports are true."

"What *did* you want here?" Val asked for the last time.

The Boss smiled. "I shall leave that mystery for you to unravel, my wounded hero. It should occupy an idle moment or two. Doubtless all will be made clear in the fullness of time. As for you," he turned upon LeFleur, "there is no use in your entertaining any foolish idea of calling the police. For our invasion today we have a court order; unhappily it is no longer of use. But we did come here in good faith, as we are prepared to prove. And all other evidence of any lawbreaking upon our part rests, I believe, upon the word of two boys, evidence which might be twisted by a clever lawyer. You may prosecute Simpson for perjury, of course. But I think that Simpson will not be in this part of the country long. Yes," he looked about him once more at garden and house, "it was a very good idea. A pity it did not work. Well, I must be going before I begin to curse my luck. When a man does that, he sometimes loses it. You must have found yours, I think."

"We did," Val answered, but the Boss did not hear him, for he had turned on his heel and was striding down the terrace. For a moment his followers hesitated uncertainly and then they were after him. Back into their sinister beetle-car went the invaders and then they were gone down the drive, leaving the Ralestones in possession of the victorious field.

"Now," Val said plaintively, "will somebody please tell me just what this is all about? Who is Jeems, really?"

"Just who I said," answered Creighton promptly. "Roderick St. Jean Ralestone, the only descendant of your pirate ancestor."

"Bettah tell us the story," suggested the swamper quietly. "Yo' ain't foolin', are yo', Mistuh Creighton?"

The New Yorker shook his head. "No, I'm not fooling.

But you are not the first one to question my story." He smiled reminiscently. "Judge Henry Lane had to see every line of written proof this morning before he would admit that the tale might be true."

"But where did you find this 'proof'?" Val demanded as Jeems pulled up chairs for the lawyer and Creighton.

"In that chest of Jeems' which you brought out of the swamp on the night of the storm," he replied promptly. "And, young man," he said to Jeems indignantly, "if you had let me see those papers of yours a month ago, instead of waiting until last week, we would have had this matter cleared up then—"

"But then we might never have found the Luck!" Val protested.

"Humph, that piece of steel is historically interesting, no doubt," conceded Creighton, "but hardly worth risking your life for."

"No? Well, you heard what that man said just now— that we had found our luck. It's so; we have had good luck since. But I'm sorry; do get on with the story of Jeems' box."

"Ah gave it to him Monday," said the swamper slowly. "But, Mistuh Creighton, there weren't nothin' in that chest but some books full of handwritin'—most in some funny foreign stuff—an' a French prayer-book."

"Plenty to establish your right to the name and a quarter interest in the estate," snapped LeFleur. Val thought the lawyer rather resented the fact that it was Creighton and not he who had found the way out of their difficulties.

"Two of those books were ships' logs, kept in the

fashion of diaries, partly in Latin,'' explained the New Yorker. ''The log of the ship *Annette Marie* for the years 1814 and 1815 gave us what we wanted. The master was Captain Roderick Ralestone, although he concealed his name in a sort of an anagram. After his quarrel with his brother he apparently went to Lafitte and purchased the ship which he had once commanded for the smuggler. Then he sailed off into the Gulf to become a free-trader, with his headquarters first in Georgetown, British Guiana, then in Dutch Curaçao, and finally at Port-au-Prince, Haiti. It was there that he met and fell in love with Valerie St. Jean de Roche, the only living child and heir of the Comte de Roche, who had survived the Terror of the French Revolution only to fall victim to the rebel slaves on his Haitian estates.

''Horribly injured, the Comte de Roche had been saved from death by the devotion of his daughter and her nurse, a free woman of color. These two women not only saved his life, but managed to keep him and themselves alive through the dark years which followed the horrors of the uprising and the overthrow of the French rule. The courage of that lady of France must have been very great. But she was near to the end of her strength when she met Roderick Ralestone.

''Against the direct orders of the despots in the land, young Ralestone got de Roche and his daughter away on his ship. Her maid chose to remain among her people. Ralestone hints that she was a sort of priestess of Voodoo and that it had been her dark powers which had protected the lives of those she loved.

230

"Ralestone took the refugees to Curaçao, but de Roche did not survive. He lived only long enough to see his daughter married to her rescuer and to persuade his son-in-law to legally adopt the name of St. Jean de Roche, that an old and honored family might not be forgotten. The Comte's only son had been killed.

"So it was as Roderick St. Jean—he dropped the 'de Roche' in time—that he returned here in 1830. His wife was dead, worn out while yet in her youth by the horrors of her girlhood. But Roderick brought with him a ten-year-old boy who had the right to both the name of Ralestone and that of de Roche.

"Roderick himself was greatly changed. Years of free-trading, both in the Gulf and in the South Seas, had made him wholly sailor. A cutlass cut disfigured his face and altered the line of his mouth. Anyone who had known Roderick Ralestone would have little interest in Captain St. Jean, the merchant adventurer. He discusses this point at some length in his log, always concealing his real name.

"For the space of a year or two he was content to live quetly. He even opened a small shop and dealt in luxuries from the south. Then the desire to wander, which must have been the keynote of his life, drove him out into the world again. He placed his son in the care of a certain priest, whom he trusted, and went south to become one of the visionary revolutionists who were fighting their way back and across South and Central America. In one bloody engagement he fell, as his son notes in the old logs which he was now using to record his own daily experiences."

"Ricky said," Val mused, "that Roderick Ralestone never died in his bed. What became of the son?"

"Father Justinian wanted him to enter the Church, but in spite of his strict training he had no vocation. The money his father had left with the priest was enough to establish him in a small coastwise trading venture, and later he developed a flatboat freight service running upriver to Nashville."

"But didn't he ever try to get in touch with the Ralestones?" Val asked.

"No. When Roderick Ralestone sailed from New Orleans he seems to have determined to cut himself off from the past entirely. As I said, he used an anagam to hide his name all the way through the log, and doubtless his son never knew that there was anything strange about his father's past. Laurent St. Jean, the son, prospered. Just before the outbreak of the Civil War he was reckoned one of the ten wealthiest men of his native city.

"But that wealth vanished in the war when shipping no longer went forth from the port. I did come across one interesting fact in Laurent's notes covering those years. In 1861 Laurent St. Jean built a blockade-runner called the *Red Bird*. His backer in the venture was a Mr. Ralestone of Pirate's Haven. So once Ralestone did meet Ralestone without being aware of the fact.

"Laurent St. Jean was imprisoned by 'Beast' Butler, along with other prominent men of the city, when the Yankees captured New Orleans. And he died in 1867 from a lingering illness contracted during his imprisonment. His son, René St. Jean, came home from war to find himself ruined. His father's shipping business existed on paper only. Having the grit and determination of his grandfather, he struggled along for almost ten years trying to get back on his feet. But those were dark years for the whole country.

"In 1876 St. Jean gave up the struggle. With his Creole wife and their two sons he moved into the swamps. Working first as a guide and trapper and then as a hunter of birds, he managed to make a sparse living. His eldest son followed in his footsteps, but the younger took to the sea. Roderick St. Jean, the eldest son, died of yellow fever in 1890. He left one son to the guardianship of his brother who had come home from the sea. That son came to look upon his uncle as his father and the real relationship between them was half forgotten.

"But René St. Jean the second was curious. He knew something of the world and he was interested in the past. It was his custom to do a great amount of reading, especially reading which concerned the history of his own state and city. And once he was inclined to get out the old sea chest which had been moved with the family for so many years. Then he must have discovered his relationship to the Ralestones; perhaps he solved the anagram or found the pasted pages in the prayer-book—

"He was not ambitious for himself, but he wanted a better chance for his foster-son and nephew than the one he had had. So he endeavored to prove his claim to this property. Unfortunately, the lawyer he trusted was shyster of the worst sort. He himself had no belief in his client's story and merely bled him for small sums each month without ever really looking into the matter."

"Gran'pappy said he was tryin' to git his rights," broke in Jeems. "He nevah tol' mah pappy what he knowed. An' he wouldn't let anyone see into that chest—he kep' it undah his bed. Then aftah Pappy died of the fever—'long with mah mothah—Gran'pappy cotched it too. An' the doctah said that was what made him so fo'getful aftahwards. He stopped goin' in town; but he came heah—'huntin' his rights,' he said. An' he tol' me that our fortune was hidden heah. 'Course," Jeems looked at them apologetically, "it soun's sorta silly, but when Gran'pappy tol' yo' things yo' kinda believed 'em. So aftah he died Ah usta come huntin' heah too. An' then when Ah opened the chest and foun' these—" From his breast pocket he drew a wash-leather bag and opened it.

He held out to Val a chain of gold mesh ending in a carnelian carved into a seal. "This is youah crest," he pointed to the seal. "Ah took it in town an' a man at the museum tol' me about it. An' this heah is Ralestone, too," he indicated a small miniature painted on a slip of yellowed ivory. Val was looking at the face of the Ralestone rebel, as near like the water-color copy Charity had made of the museum portrait at one pea is to its pod-mate. Creighton took up the small painting.

"Hm-m," he looked from the ivory to Jeems and then to Val, "this is the final proof. Either one of you might have sat for this. You have the same coloring and features. If it were not for a slight difference of expression you might pass for twins. At any rate, there is no denying that you are both Ralestones.''

''I don't think that we'll ever attempt to deny it,'' Val laughed. ''But you were right, Jeems—I mean Roderick,'' he said to his newly discovered cousin, ''you do have as much right here as we do.''

Jeems colored. ''Ah'm sorry for sayin' that,'' he confessed. ''Ah thought yo' were right smart and too good for us. An' Ah'm sorry Ah played ha'nt. But Ah didn't expec' yo' would evah see me, only the blacks, an' I didn't care 'bout them. Ah always came when yo' were 'way or in bed.''

''Well, you've explained your interest in the place,'' Val assented, ''but what about the rival? Why did he appear?''

''It started in a blackmail plot. Your family have been wealthy, you know,'' explained LeFleur. ''But then the scheme became more serious when the oil prospectors aroused interest in the swamp. Already several men whose property bounds yours have been approached by the Central American Oil Company with an offer for their land. It would not at all surprise me if you were asked to dispose of your swamp wasteland for a good price. And the rumor of oil is what made the rival, as you call him, try to press his false claim instead of merely holding it over you as a threat.''

''The Luck is certainly doing its stuff,'' Val observed. ''Here's the lost heir found, oil-wells bubbling at our back door—''

"I would hardly say that, Mr. Valerius," remonstrated LeFleur.

"They may bubble yet," the boy assured him airily. "I wouldn't put it beyond the power of that length of Damascus steel to make wells bubble. Oil-wells bubbling," Val continued from the point where the lawyer had interrupted him, "Rupert turning out to be the missing author—"

"What was that?" demanded Creighton sharply. He was on the point of handing a small book to Jeems.

"We just discovered that Rupert is your missing author," Val explained. "Didn't you guess when you heard the story of the missing Ralestone? The family went into town to tell you all about it; that's why we were alone when the invaders arrived."

"Mr. Ralestone my missing author! No, I didn't guess. I was too interested in the story—but I should have! How stupid!" He looked down at the book he still held and then put it into the swamper's hand. "Between the pages of the prayerbook, covering the offices for St. Louis' Day, you'll find the birth certificate for Laurent St. Jean with his right name," he said. "That's a very important paper to keep, young man. Mr. Ralestone my author." He wiped his forehead with the handkerchief from his breast-pocket. "How stupid of me not to have seen at once. But why—"

"He had some idea that his stuff was no good when he didn't hear from that agent," Val explained, "so he just tried to forget the whole matter."

"But I have to see him, I have to see him at once." The New Yorker looked about him as if by will-power alone he could summon Rupert to stand before him on the terrace.

"Stay to supper and you will," Val invited. "Ricky and I discovered him for you just as we promised we would. But then you've given us Rod in return. I am not," Val told his cousin, "going to call you Rick even though there is a tradition for it. There are too many 'Ricks' complicating the family history now. I think you had better be 'Rod'."

"Anythin' yo' say," he grinned.

For the third time that afternoon Val heard a car coming up the drive.

"If this should turn out to be the Grand Chan of Tartary or the Lama of Peru I shall not be one iota surprised," he announced. "After what I've been through this afternoon, nothing, absolutely nothing, would surprise me. Oh, it's only the family."

With the impatience of one who has a good earth-shaking shock ready to administer, he watched his wandering relatives disembark. Charity and Holmes were still with them and a sort of aura of disappointment hung over the group. Then Ricky looked up and with a cry of joy came up the terrace steps in what seemed like a single leap.

"Oh, Mr. Creighton," she began when Val lifted his hand. "Let me tell it," he begged, "I've been waiting for a chance like this for years." Ricky was obediently silent, thinking that he wished to break the mystery of the author. But Jeems and LeFleur understood that it was to them Val appealed.

"Val, what are you doing out of bed?" was Rupert's first question.

"Saving the old homestead while you went joyriding. We had visitors this afternoon."

"Visitors? Who?" he began when his brother silenced him with a frown.

"Oh, let's not go into that now," Val said hurriedly. "There is something more important to be discussed. Since you left this afternoon we have had an addition to the family."

"An addition to the family?" puzzled Ricky. "What do you mean?"

"Rick Ralestone has come back," Val announced.

"Val, hadn't you better go back to bed?" suggested his sister.

"Not now," he grinned at her. "I haven't lost my mind yet, nor am I raving. Ladies and gentlemen," Val prepared to echo Creighton's speech of an hour before, "permit me to introduce Roderick St. Jean de Roche Ralestone, the missing heir!"

With an impish grin Val had never seen on his face before, Jeems clicked his heels in a creditable imitation of a court bow.

18

RUPERT BRINGS HOME HIS
MARCHIONESS

"Such a nice domestic scene," Val observed.

Ricky looked up from the bowl into which she was shelling peas. "Now just what do you mean by that?" she asked suspiciously.

"Nothing, nothing at all. It's getting so I can't say a word around here without you suspecting some sort of a catch in it," her brother complained. He shifted the drawing-board Rod had fixed up for him an inch or two. Although Val's arm was at last out of the sling, he was not supposed to use it unless absolutely necessary.

"Well, after that afternoon when you made the missing heir appear like a rabbit out of a hat—" began his sister.

"Rod," Val called down to where their cousin was busied over the stretching of the new badminton net, "did you hear that? She referred to you as a rabbit—deliberately."

"Hm-m," Rod answered in absent-minded fashion. "That cat of Miss Charity's just walked away with one of those feathered things yo' bat 'round."

"Let us hope that he returns it in time," Val said; "otherwise I can prophesy that you are going to spend the rest of the morning crawling arouund under hedges and things hunting for him and it. Ricky will not be balked. If she says that we are going to play badminton—well, we are going to play badminton."

"I think that you might help too." Ricky attacked a fresh pod viciously as their cousin came up on the terrace. He stopped for a moment by Ricky's chair, long enough to gather the pods together on the paper she had put down for them, piling them up in a more orderly fashion than she was capable of.

"Doing what?" Val inquired. "You know that Lucy has chased everyone out of the house. And now that Rod has finished setting out the lawn sports, what is there left to do? By the way, did Sam mend that croquet mallet, the one with the loose head?"

"The one that you broke hitting the stone with when you aimed at your ball yesterday?" she asked sweetly. "Yes, I saw to that this morning."

"Then what more is there to worry about? Let the party begin." Val reached for his box of pencils.

That afternoon promptly at three-thirty the Ralestones of Pirate's Haven were going to give their first party. They had lived, eaten, and slept with the idea of a party for the past week until Rupert rebelled and disappeared for the morning, taking Charity with him. He declared before he left that the house was no longer habitable for anyone above the mental level of a party-mad monomaniac, a statement with which Val privately agreed. But Ricky did trap him before he got the convertible out and made him promise to bring home two pounds of salted nuts and some more ice, because she simply knew that they wouldn't have enough.

Ricky dropped the last of the peas into the bowl and leaned back in her canvas deck-chair. "I'm going to wear green," she murmured dreamily, "with that leaf thing in my hair. And Charity's going to wear her rose, the one that swishes when she walks."

"I think I'll appear in saffron," Val announced firmly. "Somehow I feel like saffron. How about you, Rod?"

The thin, efficient, brown-faced person who was Roderick St. Jean de Roche Ralestone, to grant him his full name, stretched lazily and transferred a fistful of Ricky's peas to his mouth, a mouth which was no longer sullen. At Val's question he raised his shoulders in one of his French shrugs and considered.

"Yellow, with lilies behind mah ears," he grinned at Ricky. "Bettah give them somethin' to stare at; they'll all be powerful interested, anyway."

"Yes, the lost viscount," Val agreed. "Of course, you're really only a Lord like me, but it sounds better to say 'the lost viscount.' You'll share the limelight with Rupert and the Luck, so you'd better take that pair of my flannels which haven't turned quite yellow yet.''

Rod shook his head. "This time Ah have mah own. Ah went in town shoppin' yesterday. It's mah turn to share clothes. Youah brothah told me to get yo' some shirts. So Ah did. Lucy put them in the top drawer.''

"Don't tell me,'' Val begged, aroused by this news, "that we are actually able to afford some new clothes again?''

Rod nodded and Ricky sat up. "Don't be silly,'' she said, "we're comfortably well off. With Rupert writing books, and a lot of oil or something in the swamp, why, what have we got to worry about? And next fall Rod's going to college and I'm taking that course in dress designing and Rupert's going to write another book and—and—'' Her inventive powers failed as Holmes came out on the terrace.

"Hello there.'' Val glanced at his watch. "I don't want to seem inhospitable, but you're about four hours too early. We haven't even crawled into our party duds.''

"So I see. But this isn't a social call. By the way, where's Charity?''

"Oh, she went off with Rupert this morning,'' answered Ricky. "And I think it was mean of them, running out on us that way, when there was so much to do.''

It seemed to Val that there was a faint shadow of irritation across the open good nature of Holmes' smile when he heard her answer. "That damsel is becoming very elusive nowadays,'' he observed as he sat down. "But now for business.''

"More business? Not another oil-well!" Ricky expressed her surprise vividly with upflung hands.

"Not an oil-well, no. Just this—" He pulled Val's black note-book from his pocket. "Now I am not going to tell you that I have shown them to a publisher and that he wants fifty thousand or so at five dollars apiece. But I did show them to that friend I spoke of. He isn't very well known at present but he will be some day. His name is Fenly Moss and he is interested in animated cartoons. He has some ideas that sound rather big to me.

"Fen says that these animal drawings of yours show promise and he wants to know whether you ever thought of trying something along his line?"

Val shook his head, impatient to hear the rest.

"Well, he's in town right now on his vacation and he's coming out to see you tomorrow. I advise you, Ralestone, that if Fen makes you the proposition I think he's going to, to grab it. It'll mean hard work for you and plenty of it, but there is a future to it."

"I don't know how to thank you," the boy began when Holmes frowned at him half-seriously. "None of that. I was really doing Fen a favor, but you neend't tell him that. Do you know how long Charity and your brother are going to be gone?"

"No. But they'll be back for lunch," Ricky said. "If they remember lunch—they're getting so vague lately. Val went out to call them to dinner last night and it took him a good five minutes to get them out of the garden."

"Five? Nearer ten," scoffed her brother.

Holmes got up abruptly. "Well, I'll be drifting. When is this binge of yours?"

"Three-thirty, which really means four," answered Ricky. "Aren't you going to stay to lunch?"

The New Yorker shook his head. "Sorry, I've another engagement. Thanks just the same."

"Thank *you!*" Val waved the note-book as he vanished. "Wonder why he hurried off that way?"

"Mad to think that Miss Charity was gone," answered Rod shrewdly. ".Yo've had that board long enough." He calmly possessed himself of Val's drawing equipment. "Time to rest."

"Yes, grandfather," his cousin assented meekly.

Ricky slapped at a fly. "It seems to get hotter and hotter," she said. From the breast pocket of her sport dress she produced a handkerchief and mopped her face. Then she looked at the handkerchief in surprise.

"What's the matter? Some face come off along with the paint?" asked Val.

"No. But I just remembered what this is—our clue!"

"You mean the handkerchief we found in the hall? I wonder who—"

Rod reached up and took it out of her hand.

"Mine. Miss Charity gave me a dozen last Christmas."

"Then you left it there," Ricky laughed. "Well, that solves the last of our mysteries."

"All present or accounted for," Val agreed as around the house came Rupert and their tenant.

"So there you are," began Ricky. "And I'd like to know what you've been doing all morning—"

"Would you really?" asked Rupert.

Ricky stared at him for a long moment and then she arose before transferring her gaze to Charity. It might have been sunburn or the heat Ricky had complained of which colored the cheeks of the Boston Biglow.

"Rod! Val!" cried Ricky. "Where are your manners?" As she sank forward in a deep and graceful curtsy she added, "Can't you see that Rupert has brought home his Marchioness?"

"Now that," said Val, as he held out his hand to the new mistress of Pirate's Haven, "is what I call 'Ralestone Luck.'"